MW00637953

Sherlock Holmes
and
a
Tale of Greed

[Being another manuscript found
in the dispatch box of Dr. John H. Watson,
in the vault of Cox and Co., Charing Cross,
London]

As Edited By

Daniel D. Victor, Ph.D.

Book Nine in the Series,
Sherlock Holmes and the American Literati

Hardcover 978-1-80424-195-0
Paperback ISBN 978-1-80424-196-7
ePub ISBN 978-1-80424-197-4
PDF ISBN 978-1-80424-198-1

Published by MX Publishing
335 Princess Park Manor, Royal Drive,
London, N11 3GX
www.mxpublishing.co.uk

Cover design Brian Belanger

Also by Daniel D. Victor

The Seventh Bullet:
The Further Adventures of Sherlock Holmes

A Study in Synchronicity

Sherlock Holmes and the Shadows of
St Petersburg

The Literary Adventures of Sherlock Holmes,
Volumes 1 and 2

Other Books in the Series,
"Sherlock Holmes and the American Literati":

The Final Page of Baker Street

Sherlock Holmes and the
Baron of Brede Place

Seventeen Minutes to Baker Street

The Outrage at the Diogenes Club

Sherlock Holmes and the London Particular

The Astounding Murder at Cloverwood House

Sherlock Holmes and the Pandemic of Death

Sherlock Holmes and the Case of the Fateful Arrow

3

Acknowledgments

My thanks to Judy Grabiner for her continued
guidance and insightful comments; to Sandy Cohen
for his valuable advice; to Tom Turley, a Sherlock
Holmes pasticheur second to none;
to Peter H. Weiner for his long-time
encouragement and critical readings;
and, as always, special thanks to my wife, Norma,
for her love, support and understanding.

A note on the text: In addition to the title of the
book, all chapter and section titles, headnotes, and
footnotes were supplied by the editor.

[Frank] Norris, in basing his novels upon the life about him, introduced much autobiography into his fiction.
> --Franklin Walker
> *Frank Norris:*
> *A Biography*

"I never truckled; I never took off the hat to fashion and held it out for pennies. By God, I told them the truth. They liked it or they didn't like it. What had that to do with me? I told them the truth; I knew it for the truth then; and I know it for the truth now."
> --Frank Norris
> opening card,
> *Greed,* 1924 film,
> Dir. Erich von Stroheim
> Based on Norris's novel
> *McTeague*

American Novelist Frank Norris (1870-1902)

Preface
by
John H. Watson, M.D.

If the novel was not something more than a simple diversion,
a means of whiling away a dull evening, a long railway
journey, it would not, believe me,
remain in favour another day.
—Frank Norris,
"The Responsibilities of
the Novelist"

i

Perhaps Frank Norris's version of the murder in the South Kensington Museum of Art would have turned out differently if he had not waited six years to begin composing it. Perhaps, had he not lived in Paris and been exposed to the tedious philosophy of French author Émile Zola, his interpretation of events would have been more consistent with reality. But, of course, the late American author was only seventeen at the time of the brutal homicide, and the ensuing years offered a lengthy period for reflection and reconsideration.

I should say from the start that Norris, an acquaintance from years past, greatly admired the narratives I have written of the exploits of my friend

7

and colleague, Mr. Sherlock Holmes. One need only read Norris's caustic review of *Chronicles of Martin Hewitt*, the fictional detective stories of Arthur Morrison, to appreciate Norris's opinion of my own sketches. "If you have *not* read of Sherlock Holmes' adventures," Norris wrote, "you *may* be interested in Martin Hewitt; but if you *are* familiar with the doings of that famous amateur [that is, Sherlock Holmes], you will not find these chronicles worth their ink."*

As flattering as such praise may be from an enthusiastic admirer of Kipling, Scott, and Stevenson, I none the less must take issue with Mr. Norris's views when they so broadly distort events with which I am familiar. I refer in particular to the facts behind one of the writer's most successful novels, his 1899, darkly-powerful narrative titled *McTeague*. Its relentless plot, detailed descriptions, and headstrong characters have prompted many a curious reader to question its provenance—in particular, the antecedent of the novel's primary crime, the terrible murder of a woman obsessed with hoarding her money.

Frequently identified as the prototype is a singularly gruesome homicide reported in the 10 October 1893 edition of Norris's hometown newspaper, the *San Francisco Examiner*. Beneath the heading, "Twenty-nine Fatal Wounds," appears

---

* "Fiction in Review," *The Wave* 15 (18 July 1896): 12. [emphasis added]

the account of the grisly death of one Sarah Collins, a scrubwoman at San Francisco's Felix Adler Free Kindergarten.

According to the *Examiner*, Mrs. Collins had been savagely murdered by her estranged husband, an alcoholic lout called Pat, who stabbed her numerous times when she refused to give him any of her wages. In a final act of cruelty, he left his knife protruding from her neck.

McTeague tells the story of a woman who was also fatally assaulted. Despite some obvious parallels, however, Norris never confirmed a link between the widely reported true-life crime and the transgression depicted in his novel. Nor did he ever identify the actual inspiration for the fictional crime, which, as will soon become clear, was certainly not the kindergarten murder so many of his readers like to cite.

Because Norris devoted multiple articles to analysing the writing process, one may safely assume that had he wanted to make known the true origins of the novel, he had numerous opportunities to do so. Moreover, there seems little doubt that the strong-willed author—said by his brother Charles to have been in "the very prime of his youth" when poor Frank died from a ruptured appendix at age thirty-two—would have raised vociferous arguments (however tangential) in defence of the novel's point of view.

For my part, I knew first-hand that Norris had kept a journal of the events upon which *McTeague* was based and fully expected that, following his death five years ago in October of '02, the posthumous publication of his papers would eventually resolve the issue of the novel's genesis. But, alas, the horrific earthquake and fires in April of last year that all but destroyed the city of San Francisco likewise took their toll on the archived writings of Frank Norris, which had been stored in crates in a large San Francisco warehouse.

Though some of his stories survived, most of his letters and notes did not, including many pages said to relate directly to *McTeague*. As a consequence, the nagging question of the novel's origin seemed destined to become one of those baffling literary mysteries, like the identity of the third murderer in *Macbeth,* that will forever go unsolved.

That is, until now. It has been some nine months since the great earthquake eliminated any evidence of the origins of the primary murder in Norris's novel. It is time to unveil the truth.

ii

Contrary to general opinion, the antecedent of the crime in *McTeague* was not the 1893 murder of the scrubwoman Sarah Collins, but rather another homicide entirely, a murder which occurred some six years earlier in July of '87. Moreover, it was a crime in whose solution Frank Norris, then a seventeen-year-old art student, actually participated.

In reality, the deadly affair occurred not in San Francisco, as Norris posited in *McTeague*, but—as already mentioned—here in London at the South Kensington Museum of Art. What is more, to the surprise of no one at Scotland Yard, the murder led to an investigation shaped by Sherlock Holmes, an investigation whose details have never before been revealed.

To be fair, the aforementioned Collins murder in October of '93 may well have been the catalyst that prompted Norris to set pen to paper. For within months of the homicide in San Francisco, Norris, then a senior across the bay at the University of California in Berkeley, wrote to me for whatever memories I might have related to the mystery of the body found in the South Kensington Museum.

Always ready to help a budding author, I had made the offer of support back in '87, and I responded to Norris's request by immediately forwarding to him copies of the relevant diary pages I always maintain during an investigation. In retrospect, I should like to believe that my renewed encouragement in late '93 may have played some role not only in fostering the composition of *McTeague*, but also in advancing the development of

Norris's distinguished but abbreviated literary career.

A lack of proficiency in mathematics prevented the young man's graduation from Berkeley in '94, yet months later he managed to gain admission to graduate courses at Harvard University. Thus, it was at Harvard some seven years after the horrible crime in South Kensington that Norris presented to his new writing instructor, Lewis Edwards Gates, to whom he would ultimately dedicate *McTeague*, random scenes from his now-Americanised version of the London murder tale, which he had been developing on his own outside of class.

iii

Despite the numerous details concerning the murder that I sent to Norris—not to mention whatever facts he remembered on his own—he distorted the events of the crime in South Kensington to such an extent that I cannot imagine how my notes could have been particularly useful to him. In a word, *McTeague* represents a highly fictionalised version of what actually transpired.

Though I cannot be certain what prompted all of the many emendations, Norris's 1897 lament in the San Francisco journal, *The Wave*, offers a clue concerning his change of settings. "London had her Dickens," he wrote, "New Orleans her Cable, New

York her Davis, Boston her Howells, Paris her Zola, but San Francisco still waits her novelist." One should not be surprised, therefore, at either Norris's choice of subtitles, *A Story of San Francisco*, or of his moving the central action from London's Strand to San Francisco's Polk Street.

Since embellishing the truth is the novelist's prerogative, Norris's divergence from actual events in *McTeague* is equally unsurprising. He invented new peripheral characters like the precious older couple who discover they are in love. He expanded the backgrounds of the primary actors like that of the scrubwoman upon whom he bestowed a diverse assortment of eccentric family members; and to better symbolise his theme, he traded the coal pits of Lancashire for the gold mines of California. But most significantly, despite some flashes of humour, Norris rendered extremely depressing the tone of virtually all that surrounded the poor woman's murder.

I am not alone in recognising the gloom that permeates the fictional world of *McTeague*. Literary critics more perceptive than I have identified what they call the dark pre-determinism that dominates the novel. Such critics relate its theme to the bleak Naturalism of M. Zola with whose view of man as "*La Bête Humaine*" Norris became enamoured whilst studying in Paris. To such an extent did he reflect the French author's philosophy about the degeneration of the human race that Norris himself was sometimes called "the American Zola."

Readers familiar with my own narratives shall not be surprised to discover that I adhere to a different point of view. Though not one to criticise a fellow author for dramatizing his personal philosophy, I nonetheless believe that laying such a pessimistic interpretation upon the original murder in South Kensington caused Norris to ignore what I trust my own narrative will reveal as the most noble feature of the case.

To evaluate the intricate clues of a crime, one need not rely on the murky psychology of its causes. If Frank Norris were alive today, I would remind him that no alienist is required for deducing the truth. Yet in *McTeague*, Norris sought to blame the motivation of his murderer on the deep-seated brutishness of human nature in general and on such Zola-esque elements in particular as inherited personality traits and the so-called sexual drive.

It goes without saying that I never expected the perspective of the youthful Norris to mirror my own, yet in truth I did anticipate a more accurate rendition of the case. Rather than highlighting the alleged depravity of man, any history of the events surrounding the South Kensington murder should ultimately amplify the authentic and discernible heroism that the story reveals. But then such a selfless character trait seems quite incompatible with the grim fatalism of M. Zola that pervades Norris's novel.

With all due respect to Norris's interpretation of the crime, it is the hero of the piece who deserves an author's recognition, not the so-called victimised villain. With Norris's notes forever lost, fortune has provided me with the responsibility of presenting the true record of the 1887 murder at the South Kensington Museum. As I hope the following narrative will reveal, it is a record that rightly underscores a distinction generally overlooked by Frank Norris in *McTeague*—the role which individual courage played in bringing the drama to a close.

J.H.W.

London,

January 1907

Part I

The Puzzle

Chapter One

Murder in the Museum

I want to live as long as I can,
and die when I can't help it.
--Frank Norris
Moran of The Lady Letty

Sherlock Holmes put a long forefinger to his lips, tiptoed towards the panelled door and clasped the brass handle.

Inspector Lestrade and I stood frozen in silence.

Suddenly, in an explosion of movement, Holmes jerked open the door and pulled into the room a startled lad of seventeen or eighteen. The entire episode lasted but an instant.

Clearly surprised by his near-magical injection into our midst, the young man, who must have been hovering in the museum corridor just beyond the doorway, barely managed to hang on to the black notebook in his hand. He was a tall, thin fellow with thick, middle-parted hair and, save for the usual ravages of adolescent acne, quite handsome.

Inspector Lestrade's eyebrows shot up at the intrusion, and he pointed an accusatory finger in the boy's face. "Here now, who are you?" he demanded, stretching his short frame as tall as it would allow. "What were you doing outside our door? What's your business?"

"F-Frank, F-Frank Norris," the young man stammered, an American accent colouring his words, blinking eyes revealing his confusion. "I—I haven't done anything."

A breathless police-constable carrying a hand-written note from Inspector Lestrade had interrupted our coffees earlier that morning in Baker Street. A woman had been murdered at the South Kensington Museum of Art in the Cromwell Road, the grim message informed us, and the Inspector was seeking Holmes's assistance.

There was nothing surprising in such a solicitation. In the six years since Inspector Gregson had first invited Sherlock Holmes to join Lestrade and himself in the Lauriston Gardens murder case in '81, various detectives at Scotland Yard had called upon Holmes to help advance an enquiry.

Sherlock Holmes peered at me over the lip of his coffee cup. "What say you, Watson?" he asked.

"Care to join me in polishing Lestrade's reputation?"

Having no patients to see that day, I readily agreed, and my friend advised the constable, who by then had caught his breath, that we would be along shortly. In point of fact, within the hour, Holmes and I were seated in a hansom rattling through Hyde Park in West Carriage Drive on our way to South Kensington.

The museum itself is better known today as the Victoria and Albert, the name bestowed upon it in 1899. Though it features numerous paintings— few, one must add, as grand as those in the National Gallery—the South Kensington is primarily celebrated for its presentation of the industrial arts— furniture, clothing, ceramics, metalwork and the like. So appealing is its practicality that on various evenings its many galleries and spacious courts are kept open to provide working people the opportunity to visit.

A few minutes past noon we joined countless others filing through the imposing arched entrance of the red-brick exhibition hall. It happened to be a free-admissions Monday in mid-July, and as long as the nature of our sombre mission remained confidential, Holmes and I might easily have been mistaken for the countless regular summertime patrons who stroll beneath the elegant, domed ceiling of the cavernous rotunda. Conveniently, however, the uniformed policeman who had delivered the message to Baker Street intercepted us as we entered and indicated we follow him to avoid the crowds.

The constable led Holmes and me but a short distance, depositing us before a hallway where a pair of chairs had been positioned to keep away the public. It turned out to be a whitewashed corridor near the concrete stairwells to the upper and lower ground floors, and at its centre Inspector Lestrade, black bowler jammed down over his brow, was pacing back and forth. Though chairs had been placed at the other end of the corridor as well, a low murmur from the meandering crowds were prominent enough to muffle the sound of Lestrade's footsteps.

No sooner did the sallow-faced detective see us than he paused his aimless marching and pointed with a scowl to the gleaming, grey-tiled floor in front of him. "This is where she was killed," he announced gravely.

Holmes frowned. "Where is the body now?" He had expected the crime scene to have been preserved, careful examination being his forté.

The Inspector raised both palms in an appeal to reason. "Calm yourself, Mr. Holmes. The body was properly examined by the coroner and removed to the morgue for autopsy. All is in order."

Holmes cocked an eyebrow. *"And yet you called us in?"*

The policeman removed his hat to wipe some beads of sweat from his forehead. *"As much as I hate to admit it,"* said he, *"the investigation has become a bit more complicated than it first appeared. To be honest, it's turned into quite an extraordinary situation."*

"Pray, give us the facts then," Holmes said, pausing but a moment before adding sarcastically, *"it's not as if there's a murder scene we must rush to examine."*

Ignoring the barb, Lestrade looked about. Beyond the chairs that blocked both approaches to the corridor, numerous gawkers, their voices and footfalls filling the air, stopped to peer at the three of us. *"Let's get to somewhere more private,"* he said and taking a deep breath, pulled his hat back down over his forehead and led us into an empty conference chamber at the far end of the hall. It contained a long cherrywood table and a number of matching chairs.

Once we were safely within, Lestrade closed the door. Only then did he let the air out of his cheeks and use a finger to push up the front of his bowler. Looking both ways as if to assure himself we were not being overheard in these new confines, he said, *"Understand, gentlemen, that I just got here myself. I sent you that message before I left the Yard."*

Once more, Holmes frowned. *"Start at the beginning."*

"Right," the Inspector agreed and, producing a small notebook to verify the facts, shared his information. *"A scrubwoman was murdered last night in the hallway we just vacated. She was washing the floors when someone smashed her in the side of the head. According to the coroner's preliminary observation, she had been struck in the face though it was the single blow to her temple that killed her. The museum opened this morning at 10.00, but the body was discovered by an attendant who had arrived an hour earlier. He called in the local constable a few minutes past nine."*

"And yet," Holmes said, *"you told us you only just got here. It's now close upon one. You're usually more punctual than that, Lestrade."*

The Inspector shook his head. *"Therein lies the problem, Mr. Holmes. You see, Inspector Worthy arrived—"*

"Nigel Worthy?" interrupted my friend. *"I worked with him last year on the matter concerning the Tankerville Club.* He's a wily fellow, clever and scrupulous to a fault. Why, he was most pleased when I was able to clear Major Prendergast of the*

---

* Watson describes Holmes's involvement in the Tankerville Club Scandal in the case titled "The Five Orange Pips."

charges against him. 'Justice has been done,' Worthy said."

"The very same," Lestrade replied. "Worthy was the detective assigned to the case once the local constable summoned help from the Yard. As you said, Mr. Holmes, Worthy is good at his job. He questioned the attendant who found the body, and then he called in the coroner. The body was removed not long after it was examined, and before I ever got here, the director ordered his attendants to clean up the blood. He didn't want to shock the museum's visitors. That's why no guard has been posted."

Holmes exhaled loudly.

"Come now, Mr Holmes. I appreciate your frustration, but if it's the corpse you wish to see, you can always view the remains in the city morgue."

"Not the same," said Holmes, shaking his head. "You know my methods, Lestrade. A body must be viewed in its original position. There are blood spots and footmarks to observe—not to mention the intangibles—the lingering smells, the disruption of dust, the folds in the clothing."

"And yet," I remarked, raising a finger to tick off each item, "a dead body, the police summons, the coroner's examination—you must admit, Holmes, that however awful the crime, it all sounds fairly routine."

"Watson is quite correct, Lestrade. It does sound routine. And yet just moments ago, you

referred to the situation as 'extraordinary.' Dare one ask what makes it so?"

The Inspector pursed his lips. "Only this: When Worthy returned to the Yard, he told the Chief Inspector that he knew the victim."

"Well, well," Holmes said, arching his bushy brows.

"I see you understand the state of affairs, Mr. Holmes. I can tell you that it didn't take long for word to reach Commissioner Monro, the head of C.I.D., and then go up the chain. No time at all. Before mid-day, Sir Charles Warren himself had removed Nigel from the case. Worthy couldn't be objective, Sir Charles said. And that was it then."

"That was what?" Holmes demanded. "What happened next? No doubt the consequences of Worthy's removal form the true essence of the issue."

Lestrade nodded. "Worthy reacted to his dismissal with anger. He shouted at both Gregson and me. I must say, it was rather surprising. He's usually a most temperate fellow. We tried to settle him down, but he pushed past the both of us and stormed out of the Yard. Nearly knocked me over, he did."

"Strange," Holmes murmured.

"To make matters worse, he had with him the notes he'd written during his examination of the murder. Gregson agreed to go round to Worthy's

flat to collect them once he reckoned Worthy had time to calm himself. In fact, Gregson's probably there right now. Monro ordered me to take over the proceedings here at the museum."

Sherlock Holmes shook his head.

"To be fair, gentlemen," Lestrade continued, "I've been here long enough to have learned a few things." He looked down at his notebook again. "The director reported that the dead woman lived in an attached room provided by the museum. Called herself Jane Smith, she did—not that we believe that was her real name. But with no clues to be found as yet, Mr. Holmes, I reckoned that you would be just the person to help set matters right."

Holmes offered a wry smile, then suddenly tilted his head, his attention focused on something just outside the room—a noise? a movement? It was at that moment that he tiptoed towards the door and, like a cat, commenced the quick action which, as I have already reported at the outset of this narrative, resulted in the young American's being swept into our midst.

Chapter Two

The Young Man's Story

I think you may safely set it down as a rule that
a true artist always does better than he thinks he will
but never so well as he thinks he can.
--Frank Norris
"Artist's Work"
(Theme at Harvard)
December 21, 1894

"I—I'm touring London with my family,"
Frank Norris answered Lestrade with a nervous titter.
A shorter laugh followed as the lad was apparently
gaining in a struggle to sound assertive.

"Doing *what* outside our door?" Lestrade
demanded once again.

The young man avoided the question.
Instead, he announced with increasing authority,
"You should know that my father is B.F. Norris.
He's a businessman—a jeweller."

"And just what bearing does that have on the
matter?" Lestrade wanted to know.

"I'm trying to tell you what I'm doing here.
That's what you asked. I'm an art student, you see.
I began studying when I was fifteen—at the
California School of Design in San Francisco. We'd

moved from Chicago. My father decided the warm weather out west was better for his bad hip."

Lestrade began to rock back and forth, showing no interest in an account of Norris's artistic endeavours or the physical disabilities of the young man's father.

"Let him continue," Holmes said.

Lestrade rolled his eyes, but pulled out a chair for the lad and pointed to it.

Young Norris carefully placed his black notebook on the table, seated himself, and looked up at the three adults confronting him. "My father," he said softly, "has never been particularly enthusiastic about my interest in art— not manly enough for him, I guess, or practical. 'Thimble-head bobism,' he calls it."

"Why am I not surprised?" Lestrade muttered.

"Still," Norris said a bit louder, "I must have showed some promise because a few of his friends convinced him that if I am to accomplish anything at all in the field, I should be studying in London or Paris. So it was arranged that I enrol here at the School of Art and Design."*

---

  * As a seventeen-year-old art student in 1887, Frank Norris remained some years away from discovering that his primary talent lay in writing rather than in the visual arts. In fact, it would take more than a decade for him to gain international prominence.

"Were you to travel alone?" I asked.

The lad shook his head. "My father had planned to bring me to England by himself."

"You said, '*had* planned,'" Holmes pointed out. "What changed?"

"Well," Norris replied, patting down his hair, "studying in South Kensington was the original plan. My father was going to leave me in London and tour the Continent on his own. He does that sort of thing. But then my brother, Lester—he's ten—I mean, *was* ten—he died last month—diphtheria—and obviously we had to change our schedule." Norris swallowed hard and laid both his hands on the table.

"Take your time," I advised him.

The young man spent a moment composing himself, then straightened up. "The rest of the family—my mother; my kid-brother, Charles; and my cousin, Ida—they decided to join my father and me, and Paris seemed a better fit for them than London. The trip became a diversion—especially for my mother—a way to get past what happened to Lester."

Suddenly, Norris grew silent, and sympathising with the lad's distress, Holmes, Lestrade and I allowed him his privacy. It took a few moments before he was ready to continue.

"In a week or so," he said at last, "we'll be moving on to France. If you want to know the truth, I think my father's already packed his suitcase.

31

Instead of studying here"—he swept his arm as if to include the entire South Kensington institution in his domain, "I'll be going to the *Académie Julian* in Paris." He paused to take a breath, then added proudly, "It's not a step down, you know. I shall be studying under the artist, William Bouguereau."

Whilst Lestrade clenched his teeth, clearly unhappy that Norris's explanation was drifting ever farther from the topic of the boy's presence outside our door, I felt pleased at recognizing—if not appreciating—the mentor Norris had mentioned. At a recent exhibition in the National Gallery, I had observed many a Bouguereau rendering of nubile nymphs and cavorting nudes.

A bit too prurient for my taste, I am afraid. The Frenchman's paintings might be hanging in the most exclusive museums here in London and Paris, but I know that throughout the rest of the world, not a few of his works grace the walls of pubs and men's social clubs. Still, while Bouguereau might not be my own first choice for an art instructor, his technical proficiency cannot be denied.

(No less an art *aficionado* than the eccentric Thaddeus Sholto, whom we were to meet a few months later in the case I called *The Sign of Four,* praised the "modern French school" in general and the paintings of Bouguereau in particular. Indicating the Bouguereau mounted on his own wall, Sholto

32

boasted that there could not be the least question of its authenticity.)

"Enough of this talk about art!" Lestrade shouted, announcing in no uncertain terms that his patience had run its course.

Norris shrugged. "I'm answering your question. You asked me what I'm doing here—in London."

"Not in London!" Lestrade exclaimed, his face turning red. *"Here!"* he pointed to the floor. "Here—in this building—now!"

By then, young Norris had composed himself enough to give a direct answer. "I happened to be in the museum this morning right after it opened. One of your bobbies was at the entrance to the hallway that's just outside this door." Norris motioned behind him with a flick of his head. "Everyone notices when the police are around. Who wouldn't?

"When I got closer, I saw a woman's body on the floor and a detective bending over her. Even in a plain suit," Norris smirked, "you police—with your long coats and derby hats—are easy to spot."

Not words to placate Lestrade, I thought.

"Still," the lad went on, "it was all very intriguing, and that's why I was standing by the door here—to see if I could learn anything else."

"Eavesdropping's more like it," Lestrade grumbled.

But Norris was not yet finished. "I should also tell you that I've had lots of practice drawing still lifes—you know, fresh vegetables, dead fish, marble statues—so when I saw the body on the floor, I decided to draw the entire scene." He pointed to his notebook as confirmation. It was, in fact, a sketchpad.

Holmes smiled appreciatively before simply holding out his palm. The lad thought for a moment, then handed the book over. As soon as Holmes had possession, he placed it on the table and began flipping through the pages.

Over my friend's shoulder, I could see a number of precisely-drawn renderings done in dark pencil—the first few, the muscled heads and rumps of horses; the following group, various pieces of medieval armour. The pages containing the armour were headed "Clothes of Steel," and one could not help noticing at the bottom of those illustrations the audacious signature of the artist—"Norrys"—spelled with that medieval-looking *ys* at the end.

Only after leafing through any number of hauberks, helmets, and shields did Holmes arrive at what he had been seeking—the drawing of the corpse. Like the others, this rendering in pencil had employed black, white and shades of grey, yet the content was so very different. Figures at the edges may have been lightly sketched, but the drama at the centre had been most impressively captured.

"Blimey," said Lestrade, who had been peering over Holmes's other shoulder. Straining to have a longer look, he said admiringly, "Good as a photograph, ain't it, Mr. Holmes?" And he rubbed his hands together in appreciation.

The drawing depicted the unfortunate scrubwoman lying face-down on the tiled floor. Her thick, black tresses—interrupted here and there with streaks of grey—were splayed Medusa-like over the back of her head and shoulders. Blood from her right ear oozed down her cheek to the tiles. Her dress was dark, and the edges of an apron peeked out from beneath her. At her side stood a small bucket and floor brush. Norris had depicted in meticulous detail the narrow, wooden staves of the bucket and the thick, rigid bristles of the brush. Just beyond the body, their presence less defined than that of the dead woman, loomed the imposing figure of Inspector Nigel Worthy along with a shorter, uniformed police-constable.

"All drawn with my HB pencil," Norris said, holding up the navy-blue instrument which he had fished out of a pocket.

As if in response, Sherlock Holmes withdrew a magnifying glass from inside his coat and proceeded to examine the sketch more closely. As might be expected, he spent most of his time on the body. Save for an occasional murmur of approval, silence reigned.

At last, Holmes looked up and addressed the young man. "An excellent re-creation, assuming, of course, that it reproduces all that the original scene had to offer."

"Oh, it does, Mr. Holmes," Norris said confidently. "I assure you."

"Even the poor woman's hand?"

"Especially her hand," Norris answered.

Both Lestrade and I took second looks. Neither one of us had previously noticed what had caught Holmes's attention. Though the dead woman's right hand lay out of sight beneath her body, her left hand had struck the floor near her head when she had fallen. At first glance, her fingers seemed to be curled into a fist. Upon closer examination, however, I discerned greater detail. The unfortunate woman's fingers were not curled—at least, not the middle and ring digits. In point of fact, those two fingers were missing.

Lestrade whistled at the sight. We all recognised that—assuming the accuracy of a competent coroner—such a detail would be noted in the autopsy, but now Lestrade would not have to wait for a medical report in order to begin his investigation.

Holmes noted the pale smoothness of the finger stumps. "No discoloration?" he asked the lad.

Frank Norris shook his head.

"Amputated below the lower knuckles," Holmes said, "but not too recently." With reluctance, he took his eyes off the paper and turned towards the policeman. "I suggest you survey the local hospitals, Lestrade. See if any surgeons recall a pair of finger-amputations performed some months ago. It could help establish our victim's true identity. Notify me at Baker Street if you discover anything of importance."

"Right you are, Mr. Holmes," said Lestrade, straightening his bowler. "I reckoned there'd be some advantage to calling you in."

Holmes turned back to Norris. "May I hold on to your drawing?" he asked. "At least, until the crime is solved?"

The lad furrowed his brow. He seemed hesitant to give up his artwork. "I'm not sure," he said. "I like to keep my drawings."

"I'll be certain it is returned."

The attentive reader might well wonder why any young man would avoid the chance to aid a sleuth with the reputation of Sherlock Holmes, but a reference to the calendar should put one's mind at ease. Early 1887 was rich with cases for Holmes, rich enough to distract him from the ill-advised practices with which he too often filled his free time in those early years. "The Paradol Chamber," "The Camberwell Poisoning," and "The Reigate Squires" are but a few of the cases in '87 that come to mind—

and yet it must be remembered that by the summer of that year, not one of my literary sketches had appeared in print.[*]

Still months away was the 21st November appearance of *Beeton's Christmas Annual* containing *A Study in Scarlet*, the first of my published accounts of Holmes's adventures—a report of his investigation into the Lauriston Gardens murder to which I have already referred. In short, there was no reason for Frank Norris to have any appreciation of the accomplishments of Sherlock Holmes.

As one might expect, therefore, it required a few moments for the artist to consider my friend's proposal. "Well," he drawled at last in that casual American way, "I guess it'll be all right—as long as you're sure I'll get my drawing back."

"I give you my word," Holmes replied.

"Okay," said Norris, "but first you must let me sign it." He leaned in towards Holmes and used his pencil to carefully inscribe his proper signature, not its "medieval" construction. "If my drawing is going to be shown around, I want my real name attached." He pointed the pencil at Holmes. "Good advertising principle, you know. My father's taught

---

[*] Watson's narrative, "The Reigate Squires," was published in 1893. At the time of his writing *A Tale of Greed*, however, he had yet to complete his account of the other two cases mentioned above as well as that of a number of others investigations, all referenced in "The Five Orange Pips."

me that much. Okay," he said again and watched Holmes carefully detach the page.

Only after my friend handed the sketchbook back to Norris did the young man allow himself a smile. "I can hardly wait to tell my mother," he crowed.

Chapter Three

What the Surgeon Had to Say

[Strike] but the right note,
and strike it with all your might,
strike it with iron instead of velvet,
and the clang of it shall go round of the nations.
--Frank Norris
"The Responsibilities
of the Novelist"

*L*ater in the day, Inspector Lestrade sent a second message to us at Baker Street. On this occasion he announced that the police had discovered the source of the finger amputations. Performed by Doctor Thomas Whitby, the surgery had taken place four months earlier at the Royal Brompton Hospital in Chelsea, a fifteen-minute walk from the room near the art museum that had been tenanted by the murdered woman. "Dr. Whitby has some useful information to share," Lestrade had written.

"At last," Holmes said, putting down the note, "some actual facts."

Within minutes we were once again driving across the city, this time via Park Lane and round Hyde Park to the red brick and white limestone of the large, E-shaped hospital in the Old Brompton Road.

As a work place, the Royal Brompton was not unknown to me. Before establishing my own practice, I had served there as *locum tenens*. Though I had never met Thomas Whitby, I do know that, whilst chiefly administering to pulmonary patients, the hospital offers relief for all manner of suffering.

Upon arriving, Holmes and I were directed down a long corridor to Whitby's office. Even though we confined our walk to the administrative wing, the acerbic hospital smell of carbolic acid employed in the clinics stung the senses. Fortunately, Lestrade had told the surgeon to expect us, so Holmes's knock on the door elicited immediate entry.

We crossed the threshold and found ourselves standing on plush, red carpeting in a distinguished, oak-panelled room. A stern portrait of the seventeenth-century physician, William Harvey, dominated one sidewall whilst a ceiling-high, oak bookcase filled the other. The shelving contained an impressive collection of leather-bound medical books whose musty library smell overpowered the pungent odour I feared would follow us in.

At the centre of the chamber stood a broad, highly polished mahogany desk. From the red-leather turning chair behind it, Dr. Thomas Whitby, a middle-aged gentleman dressed smartly in brown tweed, rose to greet us. His *pince-nez*, short beard, and greying black hair presented a professorial look.

"Inspector Lestrade told me you gentlemen would be coming round," he said, offering us chairs that faced his own. Once he sat down, he began fidgeting with the binaural stethoscope that lay on the desktop before him. "Truth be told," he said nervously, "I'm not used to participating in murder investigations."

"Not to worry," I cautioned. Wagging a finger between him and myself, I said, "Just consider this a professional discussion between two medical men."

Dr. Whitby nodded and offered a brief smile. "I understand that you're making enquiries about the poor woman who was found murdered at the art museum."

"That's correct," said Holmes. "The woman was missing two fingers."

Whitby nodded. "As I told the Inspector, I recalled the amputations quite readily. You see, the woman called herself Jane Smith, but one of our doctors recognised her as Katherine O'Connor, the wife of a dentist many of us know—or, at least, used to know. He hasn't been seen round here for quite some time. Maintained a dental parlour in the Strand near Trafalgar Square. Any number of my colleagues—not myself, of course—the younger ones, I mean—have shared a pint with 'Doc' O'Connor—as he liked to call himself."

The name sounded familiar. "A moment," I said. "Are you talking about Mr. Liam O'Connor who has a dental parlour near Craven Street? The place with the large gold tooth hanging in a bow window?"

"A molar, actually," Whitby said, underscoring the correction with a tap of the stethoscope. "But, yes, that's the fellow."

Small wonder I recognised the name. "Why, he pulled a back-tooth for me some time ago." I rubbed my jaw at the painful memory. "It was giving me trouble, and seeing that giant gold tooth as I walked past made me decide right then to go in and have it out. The fellow had a massive physique, as I recall. Blond curls, thick moustache, square jaw, dressed in a white smock."

"The same," Whitby agreed.

"Funny though," I said. "Now that I think about it, I remember that his blue eyes seemed rather vacant. It gave me pause. Still, with those broad shoulders and powerful arms, he looked quite the strongman."

"I'm told he worked in a coal mine as a child," Whitby offered. "That sort of labour is bound to build one up that way."

"You know," I said, stifling a laugh, "people say he's so strong that he's extracted teeth with his bare fingers." I eased my tongue into the empty spot and pulled a face. Yet I could not complain. "He did a fine job for me—with bayonet forceps, I should add, not his fingers."

Whitby flashed a grim smile. "And yet notwithstanding your vote of confidence, Doctor, he no longer maintains that office. At some point, he gave up his practice."

"For what reason?"

Whitby shook his head. "No reason given, and no one knows why. Something wrong with his licence, I believe, but the matter remains unclear. From what people said, O'Connor had little money saved, and as you might well imagine, his life went quickly downhill after his patients stopped coming. Curious though," Whitby added with a stroke of his trim beard, "it was rumoured that his wife had come into some sort of inheritance. Yet she wound up working as a scrubwoman, and as their situation deteriorated, we heard that he'd left her."

"An inheritance, you say?" Holmes drummed his forefinger on Whitby's desk. "Curious indeed. But her hand—what can you tell us about that?"

The doctor frowned and fiddled with the ear-pieces of the stethoscope. "She—she came in with infected fingers. It was near the end of last year—

they were swollen, and the nails were purple. She said a dog had bit her."

"A dog?" I repeated.

Whitby put down the stethoscope and raised his hand to stop my line of enquiry. "Not to say I believed her, of course. Oh, no. She looked more like the victim of human abuse. Her fingers appeared bruised, and there were no other lacerations on her hands that suggested a canine bite—at least, not then."

"A dog?" I said again.

"I suspected her husband. That's what one does, is it not?" Whitby removed his *pince-nez* and gestured with it in our direction. "Believe me, gentlemen, I've seen the terrible damage husbands can inflict upon their wives. To put it succinctly, I believe Liam O'Connor to be a brute of a man."

"Surely," I said in disbelief, "you're not suggesting that it was the dentist who bit her."

The surgeon shrugged. "There were no rips or tears from an animal attack, Doctor. Perhaps the man had got too rough with her. She certainly had additional bruises to suggest such brutish behaviour. In any case, by the time she arrived here for a second visit, her fingers appeared gnawed to the bone. A pair of them were too far gone to save; amputation was the only solution."

"My word," I muttered.

"An ugly business," Holmes agreed. "But her husband aside, is there anything else you can remember about the woman herself?"

Dr. Whitby furrowed his brow. "Only that she couldn't pay her service fees. Think of it, gentlemen—the wife of a dentist and she couldn't pay for services."

"A *former* dentist," I reminded Whitby.

"Not to mention," Holmes remarked, "the inheritance to which you referred."

The surgeon shook his head. "I never saw any evidence of that money. Still," said he, holding his head high as he spoke the words, "whatever the cause, here at the Royal Brompton we treated her as a charitable case." He hesitated a moment, then added, "Even though I repeat the common gossip that she has—or had—sufficient funds to pay for her expenses."

"Something we'll have to look into, eh, Watson?" Holmes said. Then with a nod, he got to his feet. "Thank you, Dr. Whitby. You've been most helpful."

Whitby replaced his *pince-nez* and rose to his feet. "Good luck to you, gentlemen. Whoever killed that poor woman should not be allowed to roam the streets of London."

"Not the streets of any city," Holmes replied as we made our way out of Whitby's office.

Holmes and I returned the way we had come in and soon found ourselves standing on the concrete stairs of the hospital's entrance beneath a cloudless summer sky. So inviting did the sun-drenched expanse of the Cromwell Road look that in spite of— or, perhaps, because of—the gruesome details we had just learned from Dr. Whitby that July afternoon, Holmes and I decided to return to Baker Street on foot. As we set out, I could not help noting that the brighter the day, the darker the direction the case seemed to be taking.

Chapter Four

Inspector Gregson's Story (I)

He's the kind of man that gets up a reputation
for being clever and artistic by running down
the very one particular thing that everyone likes,
and cracking up some book or picture or play
that no one has ever heard of.
--Frank Norris
The Pit

*T*he following morning, Billy, our boy in buttons, came racing to our door. "Policeman to see you, Mr. Holmes," he said puffing out his chest. "Inspector Gregson."

Holmes gestured for Billy to direct the visitor up the stairs.

Moments later, Inspector Tobias Gregson entered our rooms, the same Tobias Gregson who had requested Holmes's advice in the Lauriston Gardens murder case years before. Holmes had regarded him then as "the smartest of the Scotland Yarders," a belief that I reckon Gregson shared himself. To be accurate, however, it must also be remembered that Holmes referred to the entire group of C.I.D. detectives as "a bad lot."

49

Sporting a light-blue cravat and a tan summer suit, the tall policeman with the pale complexion and ash-blond hair strode through our doorway and shook hands with both of us.

Holmes ushered him to a wing chair opposite ours, and I offered Gregson a cigar.

"Don't mind if I do," he said, taking one from the box I held out to him. With an appreciative smile, he sniffed the cigar approvingly. "Nothing like a good Trichie," he said.

I agreed and had one myself whilst Holmes selected his cherrywood pipe. The clipping of cigars and the tamping of pipe tobacco followed, and soon an aromatic *mélange* of pipe and cigar smoke encircled us. I waved my arms about to clear the air of the blue haze that filled the room, but in the end I resorted to opening a window. The yellow-brick building across the road bounced the sun back in my face, and I was happy to resume my seat in the relative shade of our sitting room.

The Inspector took a long pull on the Trichinopoly and exhaled a robust cloud of smoke. "I must inform you," he began, holding the cigar off to the side, "that Tobias Gregson is here on official business."

I should explain that, strange as it may sound, the policeman had the singular habit of periodically referring to himself in the third person. The eccentricity was especially pronounced when he dealt with particularly delicate matters. Whilst frequently off-putting, the quirk none the less signalled that important information was soon to follow. On this occasion, neither Holmes nor I was disappointed.

Gregson took another puff and said, "The murder at the South Kensington Museum—Lestrade suggested I inform you of the latest developments. I immediately agreed since I know of your keen interest in peculiar cases, Mr. Holmes."

Sherlock Holmes nodded impatiently.

"Let me say at the start that I'm the copper whom yesterday afternoon the assistant commissioner chose to look into the actions of Inspector Worthy. By that I mean, the A.C. asked me to retrieve whatever information concerning the murder Worthy had collected before he was removed from the case. As you've been made aware, Nigel knew the victim—though, of course, that doesn't mean he is under any sort of suspicion."

"I should think not," I said.

"I went round to the lodging house in Camden Town where Nigel lives," Gregson reported, "but he was nowhere to be seen. The woman who owns the place let me into his rooms, and I had a look round. She said that though he'd rushed out, he did manage to tell her on the fly that he might be gone for a few days. Now before you ask, gentlemen—no, he didn't tell her where he was going. Nor did I find any sign of his notes."

"Nothing else?" Holmes asked.

"Yes, Mr. Holmes, there is something else, a most disconcerting fact. The old Punch cigar box in which Nigel stores a pistol—a .476 Enfield, if I'm not very much mistaken—was out on a table. The box was open and, I hesitate to report, empty."

Holmes inhaled the smoke from his pipe, closed his eyes, and exhaled ceilingward. Those unfamiliar with his habits might fail to note that he was paying strict attention.

Holmes and I sat quietly; Gregson regarded his cigar. Cries from street vendors wafted up through the open window and penetrated the silence.

The Inspector had another puff. "Now the story becomes a bit tricky." He resettled himself in his chair before adding, "You see, I've come to the part about Tobias Gregson's personal relationship with Nigel Worthy."

Holmes opened his eyes.

One could not overlook the red flush that coloured Gregson's face.

"Your own relationship, you say?" My friend leaned forward to take in Gregson's words.

"Look," the Inspector said, "I won't deny that many of my colleagues are envious of my skills. I'm sure you've heard some of the bitter comments Lestrade himself has made about my work."

Gregson's charge reminded me of Holmes's assessment of the two detectives. "Jealous as a pair of professional beauties," he had described the duo.

"Of course, that's the green-eyed monster talking," said Gregson, apparently seeking to drive away any thoughts on our part that he was stung by the rivalry. "To be envied by your colleagues—why, it's a compliment of sorts, really. In any case, my differences with fellow officers—Lestrade in particular—sent me off in search of fresh faces.

"Nigel Worthy came to the Yard a few years after the Lauriston Gardens case, and I discovered that, unlike Lestrade, Nigel appreciated my talents. Neither one of us was married, and we found ourselves spending much of our free time together—sometimes at the football, other times with a pint at the Clam and Oyster."

Holmes puffed repeatedly on his pipe. "Yes, yes," he said. "But what does any of this have to do with the murder of the woman in the museum?"

"I'm getting to that, Mr. Holmes. Rest assured that these details will shed some light on the matter." He laid his cigar in the ashtray on the table to his left and stared at us. His tousled blond hair and pale-blue eyes gave him quite the youthful look. "I've already said that neither Worthy nor myself is married."

"You did," I agreed.

"Well, some three years ago Nigel came close."

Holmes busied himself tamping down the shag in his pipe. I feared he felt more gossip was coming.

"Nigel and I trained down to Brighton one weekend. We hoped to have a few drinks and find some friendly ladies, but on our first day there, Nigel met a beautiful young woman called Katherine. One couldn't deny her charms, especially her piercing brown eyes and the crown of black hair coiled high upon her head."

"A moment," Holmes interrupted. "Katherine is the true given name of the scrubwoman who was murdered at the art museum, the woman whom the surgeon at the Royal Brompton identified as Katherine O'Connor, the wife of a dentist."

"I'm afraid they're one and the same, Mr. Holmes," Gregson said, "though obviously she wasn't married to O'Connor at the time Nigel met her. As it turned out, she was vacationing with her family at the hotel where we were staying. Nigel had an interest and to put it bluntly, gentlemen—as much as I don't like to admit it—Tobias Gregson became the odd man out."

Holmes and I exchanged glances. *A major concession from Gregson.* But even more intriguing was the suggestion of a triangle forming among O'Connor, Worthy, and the woman called Katherine.

"For the next three evenings," Gregson continued, "Nigel excused himself in order to take the lady on walks along the West Pier. Each night before going off to a pub on my own, I watched the pair head off into the starry night, those serpent-style gas lamps lighting the way, the ocean crashing about below them."

"Sounds quite romantic," I observed.

"Not exactly. You see, her parents trailed after them at a respectable distance. Chaperones, don't you know. Not my style, I can assure you."

Holmes puffed on his pipe.

"Plus, it was cold by the water. But Katherine was a pretty girl, and Nigel would not be dissuaded. The glass screens at the pierhead and along the sides provided some relief from the wind, and with musicians in the covered orchestra-stand providing the entertainment, I believe that even with her parents hovering about, the entire weekend seemed magical for both of them."

"Though not for you," Holmes observed.

"No," Gregson sighed, "not for me."

"And yet," I said, "you all had to leave Brighton. The magic was bound to come to an end."

"So I thought too, Doctor. But, you see, happily for Nigel, Katherine's family live in London, and upon their return, she and Nigel began stepping out together—restaurants, theatre, and the like. Nigel spent much of his free time with the woman, telling us at the Yard of her smile, her charm, her fragrance—a hint of jasmine, Nigel said. It came as no surprise, therefore, that after a few months, they agreed to marry."

"Wait a moment, Inspector," said I. "You've already told us that this Katherine is the scrubwoman who was murdered in the museum, the woman we know to have been the dentist's wife, not Worthy's."

Holmes pointed the stem of his cherrywood pipe at me. "A broken engagement, Watson, with O'Connor lurking somewhere in the background. What's more, one must assume that the woman's soured relationship with Worthy has some sort of bearing on the South Kensington murder."

Can it be possible, I wondered, *that Holmes is associating Nigel Worthy, a detective of the Metropolitan Police, with the crime?*

"You're quite correct, Mr. Holmes," Gregson agreed. "But I did say that Nigel only came *close* to marrying. Not long before the scheduled wedding, fate played her hand. His *fiancée* developed a painful tooth that required filling. Not wanting Katherine's discomfort to interrupt their nuptials, Nigel recommended to her the dental parlour where he himself had survived the extraction of an ulcerated tooth, the parlour in the Strand by Trafalgar Square."

"At last," Holmes muttered.

"Don't tell me," I said, my tongue once more working its way to the empty space. "That is how she met Mr. O'Connor."

"You know the man?" Gregson asked. "It was indeed the dentist they call Doc O'Connor."

I rubbed my jaw. "All I can say is that he remedied my problem."

"Yes," said Gregson, "he was a respected dentist, doing well enough to maintain a small practice in the heart of the city. How to put it, gentlemen? The man was quite the attraction—successful, professional, big, and strong. In fact—there's no point in drawing it out—Katherine fell in love with him, and—"

"Do you mean to tell us," I interrupted, "that this same Katherine who had been engaged to Nigel Worthy of the C.I.D. replaced one *fiancé* with the other?"

"Yes, Doctor, that's exactly what I'm trying to tell you." The Inspector cleared his throat. "But here's the most bothersome part of the story. You see, on the day that Katherine went for her treatment at O'Connor's dental parlour, Worthy promised to meet her there when he ended his shift later in the afternoon."

Gregson picked up his cigar and took a couple of puffs. He seemed to be contemplating the direction of his narrative. "Nigel told me that O'Connor would anesthetise Katherine by means of a drop-mask, which would allow her to inhale the ether that put her to sleep."

"*Pro forma*," I agreed.

"Quite so," said Gregson. "As planned, Nigel arrived at the dental parlour after work that day. He recalled how, as soon as he'd entered, the sharp, sweet smell of the ether immediately struck him. Then he saw Katherine stretched out in O'Connor's operating chair, on her breast, the red napkin the dentist used to mask any spilt blood, the cloth rising and falling with each breath. Her ebony hair hung free of its pins; the broad hem of her navy-blue dress touched the floor."

Quite the fetching portrait, I thought. *Intriguing, actually.*

The Inspector paused for another long draw of the Trichinopoly. He exhaled the smoke as slowly as I thought humanly possible. "Now here's where the story gets murky," he said, "though 'ugly' is probably a better word. . . ."

Chapter Five

Inspector Gregson's Story (II)

A literature that cannot be vulgarized is no literature at all
and will perish just as surely as rivers run to the sea.
--Frank Norris
"Salt and Sincerity"

"*T*here is no delicate way to put it,"
Inspector Gregson said. "Upon entering the dental
parlour, Nigel believed that O'Connor had just
kissed the unconscious woman."

"Preposterous!" I exclaimed. "Surely, the
Inspector was mistaken. No doubt, he was merely
observing O'Connor at work."

Gregson shook his head. "I tell you, Doctor,
the way Nigel described it, the dentist had finished
working and was bending over Katherine's prostrate
form, inhaling her jasmine scent, his lips hovering
just inches above her own. What else was Nigel to
think? What would *you* think?"

I could feel my face flush in outrage. "You
can't be suggesting that the dentist was taking
advantage of an insentient patient. Why, it's
immoral. It's dishonourable. It's—it's downright
unprofessional."

Gregson shrugged. "No one can say with certainty what the dentist was up to," he agreed, "but Nigel reacted instantly. He pulled a clasp-knife from his pocket, pointed it at the dentist, and shouted at him to step away. Then Nigel took hold of Katherine's hand, and, still wielding the blade, waited for her to come round. When she did, they left."

Sherlock Holmes puffed sedately on his pipe, uttering not a word.

"Once they reached the sidewalk, Katherine demanded to know what had so riled Nigel. No sooner did he tell her what he thought he'd seen than she bolted to the kerb and vomited—as revolted by the drama as Nigel himself had been."

"One should think so," I observed.

"Or," Holmes remarked, "she may simply have been nauseated by the ether."

"You may be right, Mr. Holmes. Perhaps it was not the depraved scenario described by Nigel that had sickened her, for, in truth, Katherine's attitude towards O'Connor began to change."

A wry smile washed across Gregson's face. "All Nigel knew was that after a few days of contemplation, Katherine viewed her drama in the operating chair in a different light. The dentist—a prominent figure, after all, a healer who had remedied the problem with her tooth—that dentist had wanted to kiss her. That dentist had found her attractive. She felt flattered."

"You can't be serious," I said.

Gregson shrugged once more. "An infatuation developed, an infatuation which, I must say, unnerved poor Nigel. He told me that he witnessed an excitement bloom in Katherine that he'd never seen before. And, of course, as her fascination with O'Connor grew, her interest in Nigel waned. Eventually, Katherine and the dentist began stepping out together."

"Incredible," I found myself saying.

"Indeed, Doctor. First Nigel, then O'Connor—big, strong men seemed to appeal to the woman. In the end Katherine told Nigel she could no longer remain engaged to him. And without another word, Nigel gave her over to the dentist."

"Quite surprising, really," said Holmes, "given what you've told us about Worthy's temper."

"I see your point, Mr. Holmes," said Gregson, "but I believe the poor fellow had simply become disenchanted. 'What else can I do?' he asked me. 'She wants to marry O'Connor. I am no longer in the race.'"

"It sounds to me," I said, shaking my head, "that he submitted rather easily. In my own experience—however limited—I find men not so quick to give up the woman they hope to marry.

"Can't say that Tobias Gregson would have been so agreeable either," the Inspector said.

"Did anyone even bother to ask the lady?" Holmes wanted to know.

Gregson's silence answered the question. A few moments later he said, "As Nigel told it, O'Connor seems to have considered his friend's generosity a noble act."

"Like the friendship of Damon and Pythias," I observed.

Gregson furrowed his brow.

"A Greek tale," I explained.

"Well," the Inspector shrugged, "all I can tell you is that Nigel didn't view it that way. He told me how it ate at him, giving up so charming a woman and then watching the dentist happily accept her hand. Still, Nigel attended their wedding and wished both of them the best—stiff upper lip, you know. I for one couldn't have remained so level, I assure you."

With that final declaration, Gregson stopped speaking. His silence appeared to confirm the end of the story.

"And now," Holmes intoned, "the woman is dead."

It did not require much thinking to create a case for murder. Perhaps Holmes was right to consider Worthy a suspect. "As much as I hate to suggest it," I offered, "policeman or not, Inspector

Worthy himself might well have harboured a grudge against his former *fiancée* for betraying him."

Sherlock Holmes pointed his pipe stem at me again. "As well as a grudge against her new husband," he said, "the man who took her away."

"True," I agreed, "but surely Worthy was more involved with the woman than he ever was with O'Connor, however friendly the two men appeared. In the end, it was she—not the dentist—who'd rejected him."

Holmes smiled. "As I am certain a man of the world like yourself can attest, Watson, in affairs of the heart, logic plays no role. Hatred can be just as strong as love."

"Sometimes stronger," I had to confess. "In such affairs—"

"If I may, gentlemen," Gregson interrupted, for it turned out that he had not yet completed his account. "I'm afraid that the story gets even uglier."

"Is that possible?" I asked.

"Decide for yourself, Doctor. You see, Katherine had a rich uncle in Brighton who died not long after the wedding. It was he, in fact, whom the family were visiting when Nigel first met Katherine in the hotel. In any case, the uncle left her two hundred pounds."

"Two hundred pounds," I marvelled. "That must be the inheritance Dr. Whitby told us about."

"Quite so," Holmes agreed. "And for Worthy, a new source of anger—greed—if he believed that the money might have been his had *he* been the one to marry Katherine."

"You may be right, Mr. Holmes," Gregson nodded. "Though to be fair, I'm convinced that at first Nigel attempted to forget it all—his former *fiancée*, the drama in the dental parlour, the inherited money. Submerging himself in his policework provided the best opportunity. Recall the job he did in single-handedly solving a kidnapping case."

"The diamond merchant's daughter in Chelsea," Holmes recalled.

"Exactly," said Gregson. "That was just weeks after Katherine had married the dentist. Nigel also did his best to stop frequenting any of the places he reckoned he might run into the newly-married couple—familiar restaurants and theatres, for example."

"I can't imagine that O'Connor and Katherine were that easy for Worthy to avoid," I said. "Especially O'Connor. After all, his dental parlour was near Trafalgar Square—less than a mile from Scotland Yard; one would expect Worthy to bump into him every now and again."

"That may be the case, Doctor," said Gregson, "but in the end, it was actually the other way round. It was the dentist who risked seeking out the policeman. O'Connor knew that Nigel and his mates liked to frequent the Clam and Oyster, the pub near Admiralty Arch. I happened to be there myself the evening O'Connor showed up."

"Fireworks?" I asked.

Gregson shook his head. "On the contrary, it turned out that O'Connor actually hoped to calm the waters. He wanted to share with Nigel the great discovery he had made—that between the two of them, it was Nigel who was the lucky one."

"Just how did he reckon that?" I asked.

"Well, as O'Connor saw it, the inheritance from her uncle brought out Katherine's true nature. To be sure, she was charming and beautiful, but once she gained all that money, she could think of nothing else but keeping her savings intact, of not losing a farthing. She became fixated—obsessed really—on preserving those funds.

"'She's a miser,' O'Connor explained to Nigel in the pub. According to the dentist, Nigel should have been the one celebrating because Nigel was the one who'd escaped marriage to the greedy witch. As the Americans like to say, Nigel had 'dodged a bullet.'"

"Ironic, isn't it?" I observed. "The money that was intended to give her comfort became her greatest worry."

"Exactly. O'Connor said she hoarded it all—her inheritance and whatever else came her way. He kept demanding that she hand it over to him. As the husband, let's not forget, he believed that what was hers was really his."

"But the law," Holmes said. "The Married Women's Property Act. It allows a wife to inherit up to two hundred pounds without being required to share it with her husband."

"Aye," said Gregson. "To the dismay of many a husband, most women know that law. After all, it's been in place for almost twenty years now. Katherine certainly was aware of it. She put her two hundred pounds in a bank in her own name and arranged to have the monthly interest cheques sent to her. She knew she was supported by the law, and she allowed O'Connor none of the principal. He reported to Nigel how she kept only the interest-earnings at home—money that O'Connor guessed she counted over and over again when he was at work.

"The situation got worse when Katherine decided to remove all of her savings from the bank. She told O'Connor she withdrew the entire lot in gold sovereigns and hid them away—in their flat or somewhere else—she never told him where. O'Connor told Nigel he'd hear Katherine murmur, 'Gold, gold, gold,' in various corners of their flat, but he searched all over with no luck. He would scream and shout at Katherine and who knows what else— especially after he'd had too much to drink."

"Indeed," I said. "We know about her fingers."

Gregson nodded. "Like his father before him, O'Connor could be a vicious drunk. 'You won't make small of me,' he would shout. It was one of his favourite charges. In the end, however, the law won, and he had to depend on Katherine to dole out money to him as she saw fit. And she doled out next to nothing."

"But his dental practice," I said. "Surely, he profited from that."

"Indeed, Doctor, for a while. Even so, it was Katherine who'd saved up enough to buy the large gilded tooth for her husband's window. It was covered in French gilt, nothing cheap about it. She called it a birthday gift, but I believe she figured it would bring in more patients—and more money."

"It certainly caught my attention," I said, recalling the large gold model that fronted the sidewalk in O'Connor's large bow window. "With those huge gold prongs hanging down, it was something to see. Smart advertising."

"True enough," said Gregson, "until the axe fell."

Holmes raised his eyebrows.

"Last year, there appeared in the *Dental Record* the suggestion that all dentists be required to have a professional degree in dentistry."[*]

"Like doctors," I said. "Makes perfect sense."

"Precisely. And yet Nigel told me how O'Connor's background revealed a contrary history. O'Connor, you see, grew up somewhere in Lancashire. His father was a coal miner—a shift boss, actually—who would come home from the pits exhausted every night—though not exhausted enough to prevent him from beating his wife or son if they got on his nerves. And not exhausted enough to drink himself to sleep."

"Like father, like son," I remarked.

Gregson ignored my observation. "O'Connor worked part-time as a car-boy in the mines, hooking mules to the small wagons filled with coal or trundling the bins himself. His mother wanted nothing more than to get her son out of harm's way. His father was drunk half the time, and the condition of the mine he was working was precarious at best. So, when her son reached his teen years and a travelling salesman came by with a white model-tooth the size of a hobnailed boot hanging at the side of his wagon, she saw an opportunity. The fellow presented himself as a dentist. Dr. Pangloss, he called himself."

"'Doctor,' I sniffed at the assumed title.

---

[*] Editorial. A teaching university. *Dent Rec* 1886; 6: 42–44.

"From *Candide*," Holmes offered with a quick smile.

"Can't say," Gregson shrugged again. "But O'Connor believed that with the right pair of pliers, this Pangloss could pull out any tooth that bothered you. What's more, the man could sell you an elixir guaranteed to make you feel better."

"A charlatan," I said.

"Maybe so, but what mattered most to O'Connor's mother was that Pangloss seemed the perfect fellow to help her son escape. She got him to agree to take the lad on as an apprentice, and one day when O'Connor's father was deep in the mines, she sent the boy off with Pangloss to seek a better fortune. I should add that O'Connor's father was killed two years later with the collapse of the mine in which he was working. O'Connor's mother died not long thereafter.

"Time passed, the lad learned his craft, and soon enough, with the help of the little money his mother had left him, he opened a dental practice in London. Never bothered with any kind of licence, though; reckoned he could do as good a job without it. But as the idea about dental degrees became more popular, people began asking which dentists had one, and those who didn't started losing business. It didn't matter that O'Connor had practised successfully for years."

"Surely," I protested, "there must be a dental board of some kind to approve one's practice—the same as with doctors."

Holmes stood up and walked to the bookshelf behind him. From an array of tomes, he pulled out a thick volume bound in blue leather. *"The Solicitors' Journal of 1878,"* he announced. Thumbing through the pages, he stopped about one quarter of the way in and read aloud: *"It shall be lawful for medical authorities to test the fitness of persons to practise dentistry.* In plain language, passing such a test earns one a licence. It's just the sort of requirement that a strict fellow like Nigel Worthy would like to see enforced—especially at the expense of a rival."

"You may be on to something there," said Gregson, "for it was an unknown person—perhaps, someone with a grudge against the dentist—who reported to the authorities that O'Connor lacked any formal training."

"Inspector Worthy?" I asked. "Is that what you're insinuating?"

Gregson shrugged ignorance. "Does it matter? With no licence, patients stopped coming. It didn't take long for O'Connor to lose his practise and the income that accompanied it. The consequences were awful. He had to give up his dental parlour— model tooth, operating chair, wash stand, and all.

"Without an income, there was no end of drunken pleas to Katherine for the gold she had hidden away. They could live for quite a while on her two hundred pounds, O'Connor told her. But Katherine—apparently, more in love with her savings than with her husband—wouldn't succumb, and soon the two of them were forced to move from their spacious digs to a cramped, one-room flat. 'A stinking rat-hole,' O'Connor called it. Sold all their furniture in an auction, right down to the carpeting."

"And still Katherine wouldn't contribute?" I asked.

"No. Nigel could only imagine the threats she had to put up with. O'Connor did hold a job with a dental-instruments company for a while, but his long-time interest in ale cost him his position. That's when Katherine took the scrubwoman's job at the museum. Why, she wouldn't even give him bus fare when he went searching for work. Told him to walk, she did, even in the rain."

What anger must have burned within the dentist, I thought. *'You won't make small of me,'* I remembered him charging.

"The man became a wreck. Neither begging nor beating helped him get what he wanted—you already know about her fingers. At last, he gave up asking Katherine for money; he left her instead. Said he was going back to the pier—whatever that means."

"The pier?" I repeated. "Brighton?"

Gregson shrugged again. "I'm not certain what he meant. I don't know where he was going."

"And meanwhile," Holmes said, "Katherine O'Connor continued her work at the museum and spent her free time counting her money."

"Right again, Mr. Holmes. What's more, however far the poor woman fell, I don't believe that Nigel ever got over his interest in her."

"Perhaps it was indeed Inspector Worthy," I suggested, "who told the authorities that O'Connor lacked a license."

"At the very least," said Gregson, "policeman that he is, I'm sure Nigel wants to locate O'Connor now so he can question him about Katherine's death—if not directly accuse him. For all the good it did, I pleaded with Nigel before he left the Yard not to hunt O'Connor on his own. He called the dentist low and vile."

"An accurate description," I said.

"Probably so, Doctor. But if it was the dentist who killed Katherine—"

"Or Worthy himself who did it," I added.

"—either way, the killer's much too dangerous to be tracked by one man. In any case, whoever did do her in, Tobias Gregson believes that if we can find where Nigel has gone, we will find O'Connor as well."

'My thought exactly," said Holmes, clapping his hands together.

Gregson picked up his cigar and had a final puff. "I must get back to the Yard," he said and snuffed out the last few inches of the Trichie in the ashtray.

Holmes and I rose to usher the policeman to the door.

"You've been a great help, Gregson," Holmes said.

I nodded in agreement, and we watched the flaxen-haired detective make his way down the stairs and out into the afternoon sun.

Chapter Six

Night Business

The People have but to say "No"
and not the strongest tyranny,
political, religious, or financial,
that was ever organized,
could survive one week.
                    --Frank Norris
                    The Octopus:
                    A Story of California

"*T*o hear Gregson tell the story," said Sherlock Holmes, "O'Connor and his wife spiralled into the depths quite quickly."

"Breathtakingly so," I agreed.

"As a consequence, it is through their new compatriots, the impoverished, that I am certain we shall find news of the missing dentist. No need to tell you, old fellow, that there's a culture of desperation out on the streets—a network, really—peopled by many poor souls. It is the logical place to begin our search. Tonight."

Mrs. Hudson was used to my friend's last-minute requests, and ignoring her traditional grumbles, we had little difficulty prompting her to furnish us with a quick meal.

"I'd like you to observe O'Connor's former dental parlour," Holmes said to me between bites of a beef sandwich. "You know the location."

Having been to see O'Connor on my own for that tooth extraction, I did indeed—though now I could not disassociate the place from the sordid tale that Gregson had recounted about the unscrupulous dentist. Yet for what purpose I should be going there on this night I could only guess.

"I suspect that there is nothing to discover," Holmes said, "but one can never tell. Katherine visited her husband's workplace, so—however unlikely—it might be the very spot where she hid her gold."

"Where the man who wanted it most would never think to look," I said, contemplating the ingenuity of such a plan.

"Precisely," Holmes said with a wry smile. "Then again, even if it is the right place, whoever killed her may have already found it. Mind you, the villain doesn't have to be her husband just because he worked there—merely some greedy miscreant who understood that Katherine had reason to frequent the dental parlour and that she might have stashed the money inside."

"Inspector Worthy comes to mind," I offered.

"I'll be on similar reconnaissance elsewhere," Holmes said cryptically. "Let us meet later tonight by Nelson's Column in Trafalgar Square—say, ten o'clock?"

I nodded approval of the location since it was so close to O'Connor's former dental parlour and after finishing my sandwich, donned wool suit and bowler for protection against the late-night chill. Minutes later, with Holmes escorting me to the door, I popped one of Mrs. Hudson's chocolate biscuits into my mouth and commenced my role as amateur detective.

A hansom deposited me just beyond Craven Street in the west end of the Strand. Beneath an evening sky beginning to darken, I confronted what used to be Mr. O'Connor's place of work.

In its current iteration, the rooms that once served as a dental parlour now housed an unassuming toy shop. Oh, the giant tooth continued to hang bigger than life inside the deep bow window, but thanks to the lighting, one could easily see that the expensive French gilt had not only been covered over with whitewash, but also adorned with an exaggerated, clownlike face complete with broad, smiling lips and huge, saucer-like eyes. Furthering the anthropomorphic display, tiny, blue trouser-legs had been painted on each of the tooth's dangling roots.

The establishment had not yet closed, and under a small sign reading "Olman's Toys" the japanned door seemed to beckon. I must confess that with its unique window of diagonally-set glazing bars, the portal appeared a more appealing entrance to a toy shop than it had as ingress to a dentist's chambers.

The high-pitched tinkling of a bell positioned at the door's top announced my presence. I remembered the walls as sterile white, but the now-warm interior had lots of dark greens and rich browns. Yet still I detected—or imagined I did—that tarlike smell of creosote one often associates with dental parlours.

What is more, no sooner did I step inside than the elderly man and woman—presumably, the Olmans—turned towards the door with frowns on their faces. Doubtlessly preparing to close for the day, they had been straightening the merchandise on the shelves. The silver-haired woman was propping up a collection of stuffed toy-bears, and the gentleman was connecting a miniature locomotive to a couple of railway carriages on a circular track. I had the distinct impression that I was intruding.

"Sorry," the old man, said, "we're closed." His hair was as silver as the woman's, presumably his wife.

Searching for signs of Katherine O'Connor's cache seemed pointless if the Olmans were shutting

78

the place down. Yet I wanted to ask about the prior tenant and needed a reason to delay them. With some degree of forethought, I might have conjured an imaginary niece or nephew as the recipient of a new toy and purchased whatever my eyes fixed upon, but with no such planning, I found that the stuffed bears and model railway offered little promise.

Glancing about in desperation, I saw a number of small, carved animals standing in pairs on a nearby shelf. Thanks to their arrangement and the wooden boat behind them, I identified the creatures as the so-called passengers about to board the biblical ark. There were twin horses and lions and elephants, and shepherding them all was a miniature Noah. It was his effigy that gave me the idea.

"I'd like to purchase a figurine," I said. As soon as I uttered the words, however, I realised that I had no idea what sort of figurine to request.

Scowling, the old man awaited a decision.

Noah did not appeal to me, yet the idea of purchasing an item that I myself might actually enjoy most certainly did. "A Scottish Highlander," I announced, thinking of my native soil, "a soldier."

"We don't have any," the man said quickly. "Besides, I've already told you that we're closed."

"If you please," I replied, "just take a moment to check."

"My husband's right," the woman joined in. "We don't sell them." Apparently, a degree more sympathetic than her husband, she added, "But have a look round yourself. You won't see any Highland soldiers."

I scanned the shelves more closely now, at the same time surreptitiously searching for any hidey-holes that could have appealed to Katherine O'Connor as a place to store her savings. In point of fact, besides the ordinary cabinets and drawers, I observed nothing that looked suspicious.

I did, however, note a half-open door in the rear which I now recalled led to a second room. The dentist had utilised it as an office. As part of the toyshop, it was filled with boxes of various sorts, a storage area obviously not available to mere customers like myself.

"What about the room in the back?" I asked, wondering all the while whether these lackadaisical Olmans actually cared about turning a profit. "I could look in there myself if you're not interested."

The old man let out a sigh, put down the miniature railway carriage he was hooking to the locomotive, and trudged towards the storage room. "Trying to close up," he muttered on the way.

Left alone with the old woman, I hoped to make some progress. "I was here once before," I told her. "Your shop used to be a dental parlour, you know."

"Believe me, we know," she said, continuing to fuss with the bears. "What with the police coming by this morning, asking us questions about the dentist." She turned to look at me more closely. "Here now, you're not one of them, are you?"

"No, no," I assured her. "I was here some time ago as a patient. Mr. O'Connor extracted one of my teeth. Did you know the dentist?"

"Oh, yes," the old woman nodded. "We met him before we moved in. A very large man with a distinctive yellow moustache. Called himself 'Doctor O'Connor,' he did. Told us he'd lost his dental practice, poor fellow. Why, we were here when his operating chair was taken away. He said he'd tried to sell it before it was repossessed, but he couldn't find a buyer. Once the chair was out, the landlord had the walls painted."

"But you kept the gold tooth," I said, pointing to the bulky reproduction hanging in the bow window.

The old woman stared at it. "Not gold anymore, is it? The dentist left it up there. Had no more need of it, did he? We painted it white, put a face on it, and gave it trousers. Figured the kiddies would like it."

"Do you know what happened to the dentist?"

"He never shared his plans with us."

One of the stuffed bears fell to the floor. Though the old woman had to bend over to recover it, she continued her train of thought. "Dr. O'Connor

81

did tell me he had a wife to go home to, but he kept mumbling about how he should never have come to London in the first place, how he should have stayed at the pier."

The pier again, I thought. *A definite clue.* "Which pier was that?" I dared ask as she replaced the fallen bear.

"Dunno," she shrugged, "he never said."

The Brighton Pier, I thought of again—*where Inspector Worthy had met the dentist's future wife.* Suddenly, I found myself wondering if O'Connor— for no coherent reason I could imagine—might have gone to Brighton.

My desire to share with Holmes this bit of news was tempered, however, when I saw the old man shuffle back from the storage room with a clutch of crinkled, brown wrapping paper in his hand.

"I found one after all," he said and presented me with his discovery.

At this point, I guessed he thought that finding the Highlander would rid him and his wife of me faster than the earlier dodge of claiming there were none. In any case, from within the paper, I withdrew a red-coated, moustachioed figure made of lead. It was about four inches in height and sported a tall, black bearskin hat and a green kilt, which might have been a Black Watch tartan, but was too pleated to tell. At the waist, the right hand grasped the handle of a tiny dagger; the left, the hilt of a sword. In a word, it was perfect.

"Fine. I'll have it," I said, and slowly the man wrapped the brown paper round the figure again and placed my purchase in a small cardboard box. I paid for the Highlander, thanked the couple for their help, and proceeded out the door. The bell tinkled again as I exited, a Scottish toy soldier in hand and a reference—however vague—to the Brighton pier in mind.

The evening had grown cooler and the gas lamps were beginning to glow. Random fingers of crepuscular light streaked across the heavens as I walked the short distance along the Strand to Trafalgar Square where my rendezvous with Sherlock Holmes was to take place.

Despite its infamous reputation as a focal point for public protest, the spacious square, standing as it does just west of the spire of St. Martin's-in-the-Fields and the dome and twin turrets of the National Gallery, can be quite the charming place. Late in a summer's day after the pigeons have gone, it is a particularly appealing destination to those out for a simple evening stroll.

Between the two fountains at the centre of the square, the Nelson Monument—the fluted

Corinthian column with the statue of Lord Nelson atop its capital—towers above all else. At the column's base recline the huge, bronzed lions, sculptures cast from the cannons of the Spanish and French ships Nelson defeated.

Despite its appeal, I do not usually frequent Trafalgar Square late at night when one reasonably expects most fashionable visitors to have deserted the place. For as the night wears on, the square attracts less agreeable sorts—in particular, the lonely souls who have nowhere else to be, spectral figures aimlessly moving about or simply standing in the darkness.

Once Big Ben chimed the ten o'clock hour, however, I watched such figures begin purposely shuffling towards the far corners of the square. These unfortunates, many of whom were dressed in threadbare clothes, formed protective groups within which they huddled together to keep warm. The constables on the watch tended to ignore such congregations, yet when any of the wretches started pestering ladies or gentlemen passing by, the authorities moved the beggars along.

Observing the police prompted my concern. I was openly carrying the small parcel that contained my new purchase and feared its appearance would identify me to the bedraggled minions as a free-spending toff. As a result, I paused near one of the lions and, tossing away the wrapping, transferred the Scottish soldier into my coat pocket.

Fortunately, I had completed the action at just the right time, for at that very moment a ragged soul with a matted beard made so bold as to call out to me for money. In a stained dark shirt and torn dark trousers, a red scarf tied loosely round his neck, he stood slouched against the lower rear flank of the closest lion. A toe leaked out of one of his dilapidated boots, and the grimy hand he extended bore gnarled fingers with chipped and blackened nails.

"A coin for the poor, Gov?" he asked in a raspy voice.

One feels sympathy for those down on their luck, but not enough to render them dependent on the good will of working people. "On your way," I told the man and walked on.

"Hoi," he shouted after me, "off to call the flatties, Gov?" Then doggedly righting himself, he circled round and blocked my path.

I had information about the dentist to share with Sherlock Holmes, and yet here I was, haggling with a vagabond covered in filth. I dodged to my left, but he lumbered to his right, and we collided. He muttered an oath yet thankfully moved on.

Glad to be free of him, I suddenly froze in my tracks, for out of the darkness materialised a low but familiar voice: "Not feeling kindly towards a poor tapper today, eh, Watson?"

"Holmes!" I exclaimed, gawping at the red-scarfed beggar.

"Keep your voice down," he whispered, putting a finger to his lips.

Once again, I had been taken in by the theatrics of my friend. "What are you up to?" I asked softly.

"Beyond a little thievery, you mean?" Reaching into his pocket, he sheepishly handed over the little Highlander, which I now realised he had pilfered from me when we had bumped together.

I snatched back the soldier and secured it inside my coat. "Most unkind," I muttered through a cloud of humiliation, more embarrassed by my own gullibility than by Holmes's temporary possession of my Highlander. But then I recalled our mission, and once he resumed slouching against the lion, I proceeded to relate *sotto voce* what I had learned in the toy shop about O'Connor's mysterious flight to an unknown pier.

"The West Pier at Brighton," I went so far as to suggest.

Holmes rubbed his bearded chin. "There are lots of places with piers in these islands, Watson," he said quietly. "Perhaps O'Connor did return to Brighton. But he might have gone to Blackpool. Or Bournemouth. Or somewhere else."

Holmes was right, of course. I could only shake my head.

"What's more," he continued, "if O'Connor shared his history with your friends in the toy shop, one must assume that Inspector Worthy has also heard about the pier—whichever one it may be. If, as we suspect, Worthy knows where to search for the dentist, he—along with his pistol, I remind you—is probably already on his way. It is their mutual destination that I hope to discover."

"How?"

Still hunched over, Holmes tightened his red scarf and flicked his eyes in the direction of the people crowding together. "I intend to speak with the denizens of Trafalgar Square later tonight. There's much movement and communication among the city's lowest classes. They discuss the best doss houses, the safest sleeping areas, the worst locations for police, and the comings and goings of fellow-travellers throughout all of London. Such information is their lifeblood. To the many who wander, South Kensington is no distance at all from Trafalgar Square."

I looked about at the sullen faces surrounding us. "Be careful, Holmes. There are those who might object to your pointed questions."

Sherlock Holmes offered a quick nod. "I shall meet you at Baker Street on the morrow and share what I have learned." With those words, he adjusted his scarf, pulled at his beard, and faded into the hapless gatherings of impoverished souls.

Chapter Seven

Holmes's Account

Always blame conditions, not men.
--Frank Norris
The Octopus:
A Story of California

*T*he following morning, I was startled to see the tramp with the red scarf buttering toast at our breakfast table. He was seated in a slash of sunshine from an open window, and this illumination made his appearance all the more striking. Once I shook the remnants of sleep from my brain, however, I recalled the disguise that Sherlock Holmes had effected the evening before, and I joined my friend at the table.

Holmes may still have been wearing the bright-red scarf, but at least he had rid himself of his tangle of beard. In any case, like Hamlet addressing the skull of Yorick, he seemed mesmerised by the buttered toast he was holding high. "One takes such delights for granted," he observed with a sigh.

I assumed his activities in Trafalgar Square had put him in such a state and asked him what he had learned the previous night.

"Besides how many people suffer a lack of food?" he replied, laying the toast on his plate. "Ah, Watson," he sighed again, "life on the streets. One forgets the toll it takes on the downtrodden or the causes that send them there."

"But the case, Holmes. What did you learn about that?"

"Yes, the case. After you left, I spent my time asking the inhabitants of the square if anyone frequented the back alleys of South Kensington. I dared to hope that someone might even have known the murdered woman."

"And?"

"Most people turned away, but at least I earned a few sympathetic headshakes and 'Sorry, mate,' as I went about. Still, I continued enquiring, and at last a woman told me to wait until 'a bloke called Jib' came round. She said that he usually appeared sometime after midnight, and he might be able to help me."

"And did you find this Jib?"

"I did indeed, Watson, but before I found him," Holmes paused to pour himself a coffee from Mrs. Hudson's silver-plated pot, "I was forced to watch the unfortunate ritual in the square that occurs each night as the clock nears twelve—dark faces beneath the moonless sky, pulling round their shoulders whatever rags they have in order to keep themselves warm."

I nodded sympathetically, having witnessed much of the same myself.

"Once midnight arrives, they start settling in to sleep. It's quite a disturbing sight, actually—all those poor souls gathered together, tightly packing benches or laying their heads on the ground near the north wall. The lucky ones have something upon which to stretch out—sacking or bits of old rug. The rest lie directly on the bare flags, subject to the cold. The truly lucky have a decent coat or a wool blanket or even some old newspapers to serve as covering. Hundreds of people just lying down and going to sleep—or trying to."

"I saw the police there," I told him. "They seemed to be leaving most of the poor alone."

"Credit the local constabulary with some degree of decency. Once the chimes strike twelve, they generally look the other way. Unless under order, the police will usually move along and let the wretches be. Even so, only those people most experienced at what they call 'rough sleep' can hope for significant rest."

The power of misery, I thought. *That such activity occurs nightly whilst we enjoy a warm fire and a comfortable bed. . . .* I could only shake my head.

"Eventually," continued Holmes, "the woman I'd spoken to earlier pointed out a singular-looking fellow in a flat cap. Beneath it, wild strands of white hair shot out, and a black patch covered his left eye. He was the one called Jib. He had secured a spot for himself at the end of a long, wooden bench packed tightly with seven others, a single sheet of wrinkled brown paper blanketing them all.

"I sidled up to him and close to his ear rattled some coins that lay in my pocket. 'I need some information,' I said softly.

"He heard the jingle and because he was seated at the end, extricated himself from his compatriots without much trouble. I followed him to a distant patch where we could speak in private.

"'I'm told you're the one to talk to if I want information,' I said.

"He narrowed his one visible eye and, rubbing his grizzled chin, said in a remarkably educated voice, 'I might be of some service to you— if the price is right.' I marvelled at his elocution, but reasoned that this was not the time to go off exploring his personal history. Instead, I passed him a shilling. 'There's another for you if the information is good.'

"'What would you like to know?' he asked.

"'I'm looking for someone familiar with the inhabitants of the streets near the South Kensington Art Museum. The Cromwell Road in particular.'

"'What sort of person do you have in mind?' he asked in a tone that was so matter-of fact we might have been discussing the price of apples.

"'Someone who fences stolen property,' I said, figuring that the murdered woman—recall that we know she refused to spend her savings—would have been in need of money. 'Someone who buys jewellery on the sly,' I told Jib, 'a person one might approach to sell things quickly.'

"'Zahrkoff the junkman,' Jib said without a thought. 'Ginger-haired fellow. Buys anything he can get his hands on—old crockery, discarded clothing, small furniture—lamps and such—but especially jewellery, gold jewellery. He'll sell his entire lot for gold. It nourishes his greed. Look in the back alleys round the museum for Zahrkoff.'

"I dug into my pocket for another shilling and handed it to my informer.

"'Be careful, Mr. Holmes,' Jib surprised me by saying. 'Murder is no stranger to South Kensington.' Though I had no clue how he had done it, even in the darkness I could sense the joy he felt in revealing that he had discerned my identity."

Holmes cocked an eyebrow in my direction. His message was obvious. Clearly, this Jib fellow with one eye was more perceptive than I with two who never seemed able to penetrate my friend's disguises.

"By way of Piccadilly, Knightsbridge, and the Old Brompton Road," Holmes said, "I walked towards the South Kensington Museum. At that time of night, it required little more than a half hour.

"Constables roamed the streets, but as in the square, they tended to look the other way when it came to the unfortunates—at least those trying to sleep on sidewalk benches or in the alcoves of small shops.

"Through the murk I could hear the clopping of horses' hooves on the cobblestones as the odd carriage rolled by. Every now and again, one would stop by the streetwalkers plying their trade, the same women who turned away from me after a single glance—an advantage, I should say, to appearing destitute. The beggars avoided me as well, and the few people with whom I did converse could not—or would not—tell me anything about the red-headed man called Zahrkoff.

"As I approached the South Kensington Museum, however, I saw three women congregating beneath a gas lamp. One stood out in particular. Unlike the other two who were dressed in black and had their skirts hiked up, this one wore a striped dress of black-and-white buttoned to her neck and stretching to the ground. Upon her head rested a pointed black hat with a white feather. The closer I got, the more I could detect the scent of lavender oil.

"Dare I say that compared to her companions, this woman of the night, her cheeks free of rouge, exuded an aura of authority and sensibility that suggested she might have some knowledge of events in the neighbourhood.

"At the same time, she was eyeing me up and down. With the flick of her hand, she said, 'Off with you, mate. You're bad for business.'

"The rattling of coins in my coat pocket made her reconsider. 'There's money for you,' I told her, 'if you can furnish me with the information I seek.'

"She raised an eyebrow. My appeal to lucre had clearly got her attention and, clasping my arm, she led me away from her two associates. Crossing the road into darkness, we stopped at the entrance to a bricked alleyway that ran off somewhere behind the vague shape of the museum looming before us. She directed me to a nearby alcove in its sidewall where we could remain hidden. It was obvious she knew her way round.

"All the while, I did my share of looking about. I knew too many stories of the fancy boys for whom such women work attacking their clients for more money than the nightly trade provided. Fortunately, it turned out that we were quite alone.

"'What's that you want to know, then?' the woman asked.

"I struck a Vesta for light. 'I'm looking for a man called Zahrkoff. Do you know him?'

"In the flame of the match, I could see the look of disgust that crossed her face. ''e's a wrong'un,' she said.

"'Tell me where to find him, and it will be to your advantage.'

"'Nothing else, dear?' She pressed my arm and drew me close.

"'Just lead me to Zahrkoff,' I said and offered her some coins.

"She snatched them from my hand and, backing away, bit them to be certain they were real. Once satisfied, she guided me to the centre of the alleyway and pointed into the blackness.

"'Down there,' she said. 'At the rear of the museum there's a turning. That ginger-'aired devil lives in the first building on the left, a boarding 'ouse it is. In a flat on the ground floor.'

"I gave her more coins, and with a squeeze of my arm, she whispered, 'Don't let on that Pauline peached.' Then she disappeared into the night, leaving only the aromatic lavender scent as a reminder of her presence. Moments later, as if she had magically materialised out of nothing, she reappeared under the streetlamp next to her two companions."

"Just beyond the turning stood the house. Despite the darkness, I could distinguish a few broken windows, the odd missing shutter, and various walls sullied with bold markings of *graffiti*. Though the unsavoury place looked devoid of life, through the grime of a ground-floor window I made out the dim light of a lantern.

"With little concern about the lateness of the hour, I knocked on the outer door. No one responded, and I knocked louder.

"'Yeh?' a deep voice growled from inside.

"'Zahrkoff?'

"'Who wants to know?'

"'A friend of Jib,' I said.

"The door opened a few inches, and the stink of burnt cooking oil escaped from within. The figure in the doorway placed the lantern on the floor next to him, and in the few inches of open space I could see a short, crooked man with oily, ginger hair that fell to his shoulders. A long reddish beard covered much of his chest. He was dressed in black, and even with the help of the lantern, his image merged into the gloom that surrounded him. 'Who are ye then?' he demanded.

"'As I said, a friend of Jib.'

"He reached down for the lantern and held it high so he could see my face. '"Got a name?'

"'Got some brass instead.' I jingled the coins in my pocket.

"'What do ye want?'

"'Some answers to my questions.' I jingled the coins again.

"He murmured some animal sound of consent, so I ventured on. 'Did you know the woman who was killed in the museum?' I asked.

"'The dentist's wife? Mebbe. What's it to ye?'

"'She owed me money,' I lied, 'and I'm looking to collect.'

"From somewhere down in Zahrkoff's chest came a deep-throated rattle. 'Like ye said, she's gone. Who ye reckon on collecting it from?'

"'That's what I came to you for. I figure you know where she spent her money.'

"He looked me over and held out a greasy palm. "'I ain't saying no more till I get some coin.'

"I laid a few shillings in his grimy hand, and he smiled. "Don't mind telling ye. I done some business with the woman—that I won't deny. She was broke and sold me what jewellery she 'ad left.'

"'I heard she had money in the bank.'

"'Yeh. Once. Two-'unnert quid. But word is, she drew it out and 'id it somewheres. Least, that's what 'er man said. Every time I seen the dentist, 'e was complaining about 'ow she had this stash and wouldn't share nothing with 'im. 'Course, with 'er being dead, none of that matters any more, does it?'

"'Does to me,' I said. 'I'm still looking for my share, and I want to talk to the dentist about it.'

"Zahrkoff growled again. Though it sounded like a grumble of understanding, he had not yet told me what I wanted to know—where the dead woman's husband had gone off to. I reckoned it was time to make the villain uncomfortable. He needed to feel entangled, perhaps even threatened. 'Back in the square,' I lied again, 'people are saying that maybe a ginger-haired fellow done her in. Maybe Zahrkoff saw where she hid her money, and maybe Zahrkoff killed her for it.'

"The dark figure raised his lantern again to see me better. With the free hand, he pointed a crooked finger at me. 'That what *ye're* saying too?'

"'Got a better idea?' I asked.

"'Wouldn't surprise me none if the dentist topped 'er when she wouldn't 'and over the money. Then again, mebbe it was that copper what killed 'er, the one what used to sniff round 'er any time 'e got the chance.'

"'Reasonable theories,' I said. 'But I still want to collect my share. Where would I find this dentist?'

"'Don't know for sure," he said, putting out his palm again.

"I clasped some coins in my hand before him, and he said, 'The dentist was always talking about the pier. Talked about wanting to go back to the simpler life at the pier.'"

I struck my fist on the table. "The pier again, Holmes!" I exclaimed. "The same story I heard from the people in the toy shop. Back to Brighton, is it then?"

"Not yet. Just like you, Watson, I wanted to know which pier. But Zahrkoff merely grinned at me when I demanded the name. I gave him the coins and rattled the ones still in my pocket, but the villain simply showed me more of his yellow teeth.

"I had nothing left to ask, and he had nothing left to tell. So I tipped my cap to the rogue and told him that despite his meagre help, I was going to hunt down Doc O'Connor. 'I plan on collecting what's due me,' I said.

"'Good luck to ye,' Zahrkoff laughed, eyeing me again. 'The dentist is a giant. Take more than the likes of ye to bring 'im down.'

"I turned away, leaving the fellow at his door, and made my way back here to Baker Street." Holmes held up his toast again. "Just in time for breakfast."

Chapter Eight

Norris to the Rescue

I'm out to sea, I'm out to sea!
'Tisn't half as fine as I thought it would be.
--Frank Norris
Journal
(Quoted by Charles Norris,
Frank Norris, 1870-1902)

"*E*xcellent work," I told Sherlock Holmes as he bit into his toast. "And yet we still must ask: Where is that pier?"

As if in answer to my question, the door burst open, and in rushed Frank Norris. "Wigan!" he shouted.

Moments later, a set of footfalls rang out, and before we could understand the meaning of Norris's comment, Billy bounded in, clearly out of breath. "Sorry, Mr. Holmes," the page panted. "I tried to stop him, but he run up the stairs before I could get hold of him."

"Quite all right," said Holmes, waving Billy out. Then he rose from the table and turned to Norris, who was breathing heavily himself. "What's this about Wigan?" Holmes demanded. "Wigan is a city near Liverpool. Are you saying it's connected to our case? Is that where you think the dentist has gone?"

Norris's eyes widened. "What dentist? It's the policeman I'm talking about, the tall one who came to the museum Monday morning. He came back today, and I followed him."

"You're referring to Inspector Worthy," I suggested.

"If you say so. I watched him go into the dead woman's apartment this morning. When he came out, he hailed a carriage. 'Euston Station!' he vociferated to the driver, and before I could catch up, they were gone."

Catch up? I wondered.

"I hired my own cab," Norris went on, "and I followed him. When I got to the station, I trailed this Inspector Worthy to the wicket. I watched him buy a ticket, and I was going to go to the window and make up some story about how he was my dad and I got separated from him and needed a ticket to the same place. But one of your bobbies got there first, and I heard him ask where the previous gentleman had bought a ticket for. Wigan was the answer, and I rushed back here to tell you."

"Just how do you have money to be hiring cabs?" I wanted to know.

"My father," young Norris smiled impishly. "You forget—he's rich. I grew up in a big house in

Chicago with servants and horses and monogrammed carriages—not to mention the country home at Lake Geneva. My father figures that if I have enough to spend, I'll leave him alone. It's the same technique he uses with my mother."

I raised an eyebrow at this recital of facts, but Holmes was more interested in the clue the lad had just presented. He raised his hands to slow Norris down.

"You said Wigan?" he asked again.

The young man nodded, and Holmes said to me, "That's where we must search, Watson, not Brighton."

"Brighton?" Norris asked. "My parents took me there when I was eight. What does Brighton have to do with anything?"

"Nothing," said Holmes. "It's not the West Pier at Brighton the dentist has been going on about."

"It must be a pier in Wigan then," I said.

"But there is no pier in Wigan," Holmes replied. "At least, no real pier."

"What does that mean?" Norris asked.

"Another one of those curious incidents," said Holmes, "a joke really. The so-called 'Wigan Pier' is actually a dock where coal is transferred from rail to canal ships. Stevedores call it the 'pier' sarcastically—as if it were some upper-class, seaside-holiday venue—probably to lighten the work they put in. A vacation spot it most definitely is not."*

"I understand," said Norris.

"So, it's to Wigan that Worthy must be following O'Connor," I said.

"Exactly."

"Who's O'Connor?" Norris asked.

"He's the dentist we talked about," I explained, "a suspect in the murder. But why," I asked Holmes, "would Worthy return to the woman's flat?"

"No doubt he was looking for anything he missed on his first visit—clues that could tell him where O'Connor had run off to. For that matter, he might also have been looking for the gold his former *fiancée* had hidden away."

"I say, Holmes, you're not seriously suggesting that Worthy was searching for the woman's money. That line of thinking links Worthy to the murder again."

"As distasteful as it is, we can't reject the proposition. Worthy remains a suspect, and we also

---

* Today the city of Wigan is commonly associated with the book by George Orwell, *The Road to Wigan Pier*, an exposé of the terrible working conditions faced by miners in the Lancashire Coalfields. Needless to say, the actual "Wigan Pier," the heavily used loading dock Holmes refers to, offered no seaside attractions. In 1936, Orwell himself admitted surprise at discovering that no such "pier" in Wigan ever existed.

cannot omit Zahrkoff who knew of the money as well. As you said, we already suspect the dentist."

"Who's Zahrkoff" Norris asked.

Before either one of us could answer, there was a knock on the door. We all turned and stared at the sound.

"Come," said Sherlock Holmes.

This time it was not Billy who entered to announce a visitor, but Mrs. Hudson herself. As landlady, she reserved the right to escort to our door the most significant-looking callers.

"There's an American woman to see you, Mr. Holmes," she said, drying her hands on her small white apron. "She seems quite upset."

"Do show her in, Mrs. Hudson," said my friend.

Holmes and I both got to our feet, and I put on my coat just as a stately woman in mourning glided into our rooms. Her thick white hair was trussed up beneath a round black hat, and her statuesque frame was similarly draped in black. She was quite handsome in appearance and graceful in movement. Indeed, there was a sort of regal quality about her.

"Mother," young Frank said.

I recalled Norris's reference to the death of his brother. Small wonder the woman wore black.

"So *there* you are," our visitor declaimed to the lad "I've been worried sick about you all morning."

"Mrs. Norris, I presume," Holmes said.

"Mrs. Gertrude Doggett Norris," the woman announced, extending a black-gloved hand.

I was about to offer condolences, but she dismissed the gesture. For that matter, she also ignored the beggar's costume in which Holmes was attired. "I don't have time for social graces," she declared. Then she faced her son. "Today is Wednesday. Do you remember that we had a date to walk over to the National Gallery this afternoon?" To us, she explained. "It's very near our hotel—the Morley in Trafalgar Square." She turned back to stare at her son.

"I—I was busy," the boy offered.

"Your father," Mrs. Norris went on, "says I'm making the usual fuss. He thinks that you've been out exploring and just lost track of the time. But I remember you talked about Sherlock Holmes the other day, and I got this address from Scotland Yard."

"It is true, Madam," said Holmes, "that your son and I met Monday, but I assure you that Dr. Watson and I left him at the South Kensington Museum. His appearance here today is a surprise to both of us."

Mrs. Norris shook her head. "He told me about your murder investigation. He seems to want to be part of it."

"And a great help he's been already," said Holmes. "You've raised quite the clever lad."

Savouring the unexpected compliment, the woman seemed to relax. "Is there no way to keep him out of it, Mr. Holmes? Is there no way to keep him safe? I've only just lost one boy—and two little girls before him." Clasping her hands together, she added dramatically, "I live in the shadow of a day that has gone, a day that can never come back to me."

As her son would later explain, Mrs. Norris— when still Miss Doggett—had served a short stint as a teacher before blossoming into a Shakespearean actress. It was in keeping with her poetic background that she had echoed the mournful words of Tennyson.* For better or for worse, only after the jewellery entrepreneur, B.F. Norris, had swept her off her feet did she leave the stage.

With her hands still tightly clasped, she now announced, "It is for Frank, my living son, one of the two still left to me, that I implore you for help, Mr. Holmes. I must keep him safe."

---

* Break, break, break,
At the foot of thy crags, O sea!
But the tender grace of a day that is dead
Will never come back to me.
        --Alfred Lord Tennyson
        "Break, Break, Break"

Hoping to set matters right, I reported the drawing young Frank had contributed. "Quite the accomplished artist," I told the woman.

Mrs. Norris nodded, regaining more strength as she spoke of her son's talents. "He's also interested in writing, you know."

"But I thought his talent lay in painting," I said, intrigued by the idea of young Norris as a fellow author. "Why, the drawing he showed us—"

"While it's true," Mrs. Norris interrupted, "that my son is studying art, I view him as a *littérateur* as well. Stories swirl in his brain, and I'm afraid that the untimely death of some poor woman is the very thing I can imagine him inventing a tale about. Isn't that right, Frankie—some novel about a violent crime?"

The red-faced lad appeared too embarrassed to reply.

"Come, Frankie. Let's go back to the hotel."

The young man rolled his eyes and failed to move.

"Recall the words of the Bible, Frankie." Raising a finger to emphasise the point, she recited, "'The eye that scorns to obey a mother will be picked out by the ravens and eaten by vultures.'"[*] To Holmes and me, she explained, "The family reads the Bible together every night, don't we, Frank?"

---

[*] Proverbs 30:17

With a wink in our direction, the lad responded with a biblical quotation of his own, "'Do not provoke your children, lest they become discouraged.'"*

Mrs. Norris raised her arm to invite her son to join her and, albeit reluctantly, he did. She attempted to put her arm round his waist to shepherd him away, but the young man twisted out of her reach.

With a shrug, Mrs. Norris turned to Holmes and me. "Remember," she said, "we're staying at the Morley "You can find me there." With young Frank in her wake, she clutched at her skirt, made a sweeping turn, and marched out the door. The woman knew how to effect a dramatic exit.

---

* Colossians 3:21

Part II

The Hunt

Chapter Nine

Riding the Rails

Things can happen in some cities
and the tale of them will be interesting:
the same story laid in another city
would be ridiculous.
                              --Frank Norris (Attrib.)

I began receiving patients in my surgery at
7.00 Thursday morning. The early visits allowed me
sufficient time to re-join Sherlock Holmes in Baker
Street at 1.00 for our railway journey to the collieries
in the north.

It was beneath a brilliant July sun that we set
about hailing a cab. Bathed in sunlight as we were, I
could not help thinking that if penning a novel
instead of a history, I would have depicted the day as
overcast and gloomy. A dark and dreary sky would
better portend not only the bleakness of the
coalfields, but also the danger inherent in our
journey. In reality, of course, Holmes's request that
I bring along my Webley emphasised the latter point
quite distinctly.

Despite the bright, summery day in London,
we knew it would be cooler further north, a drop of

seven to ten degrees a distinct possibility, the nights even colder. As a result, Holmes wore a long coat and deerstalker; I, my warm wool suit and bowler from two nights before. We carried with us only our small Gladstones for what we hoped would be but a short period away from London.

The afternoon express, which left Euston Station at 2.45, was to arrive that evening at Lime Street Liverpool at 7.00. According to our *Bradshaw*, there were early-morning departures as well, but those trains stopped so often that it would have made little sense for me to give up attending my surgery in order to spend most of the day in a railway carriage arriving not much before the express.

In either case, our arrival in Liverpool would be late enough to put off the branch-line trip to Wigan until the next day. For a place to spend the night, Holmes and I had booked rooms in the North Western Hotel directly across the road from the train station.

A four-wheeler deposited us in Drummond Street, and we joined the ranks of determined travellers striding towards the imposing Euston Arch that marked the station's entrance. The hurried movements of our fellow passengers, however, did nothing to block my view of a beggar squatting on the pavement at the base of the arch. The man was dressed in black and had the same long ginger hair and beard that Holmes had attributed to the abominable wretch called Zahrkoff whom he had encountered two nights before.

One could not miss the creature; the red beard was like a beacon. Though extending a cup for money towards people walking by, he began eyeing Holmes and me as soon as we had exited the carriage. No sooner did we pass him than he rose, and remaining some twenty feet behind, trailed us past the pillars supporting the station's great iron-ridged roof and onward towards the ticket windows.

Strangely, Holmes seemed oblivious to our pursuer. Instead of calling him out, Holmes stepped up to a ticket agent at an open window and purchased a pair of returns to Liverpool. As we proceeded in the direction of the trains, a quick glance over my shoulder assured me that the red beard was still there, attempting quite unsuccessfully to blend in among the crowds of travellers making their way to or from the platforms.

"I say, Holmes, have you noticed that we are being followed?"

My friend smiled. "Indeed, Watson. Ever since we left Baker Street."

"Impossible," I replied. "The fellow had been camped outside the arch when we left the carriage. I saw him stand up and begin to follow us as soon as we walked past him."

Sherlock Holmes laughed heartily. "Oh, you're referring to Zahrkoff. Yes, I suppose we should see what he has to say for himself."

The next moment Holmes pulled up and performed an about-turn. The beggar, who by now was only ten feet behind, stopped suddenly, and Holmes marched back to him.

"What's your game, Zahrkoff?" Holmes asked.

The ginger-haired fellow hesitated but a moment. "Might ask ye the same, Mr. Sherlock 'olmes." He spat out the name. "No pocket full of coins today, eh?"

"Ah," my friend replied, "you've been talking to Jib."

Zahrkoff smirked. "Someone comes to me offering money and asking about one of my acquaintances, I want to know more about 'im, don't I? Who can tell?" he said, placing a finger by the side of his nose. "Mebbe there's still more in it for me. I told you about the pier. You're Sherlock bloody 'olmes. I expected you to figure it out— though 'ow you done it is beyond me. I expected you to be travelling to Wigan today, and I reckoned it might be on the express to Liverpool from Euston. I 'ung round to be sure."

"I'm afraid you're out of luck, Zahrkoff. Nothing more for you to learn here."

"Can't 'urt to try," he muttered. But once found out, there was no reason for him to continue following us. The beggar turned round and walked slowly back in the direction he had come.

I, however, was less interested in the departing Zahrkoff than in my friend's previous comment. Holmes had said that he knew we had been followed from the start in Baker Street.

When I asked him to explain, he replied with a singular query. "Did you not feel the slight jolt in the carriage moments before the horses started off?"

I told him I had not.

"It was quite consistent with someone leaping onto the rear of a four-wheeler to steal a ride."

I had no idea to whom Holmes was referring. "Who—?"

"Let's have the culprit explain it for himself." Holmes put down his Gladstone and turned towards one of the support columns nearest us. "You, there, Norris," he called out. "Show yourself."

Though a few people within earshot stopped to stare at whom the man in the deerstalker might be shouting, no one emerged from behind the pillar. After another moment, Holmes himself marched over and pulled from behind it the American lad with whom we had become acquainted during the last few days. With a firm hand on the grey haversack that hung from the lad's left shoulder, Holmes steered young Norris back to me.

Now I understood what the lad had previously meant by "catch up." Unlike his following of Worthy, on this occasion Norris had had the opportunity to grab onto the rear of our carriage and hold on until we reached our destination.

"Who was that man you were talking to?" Norris asked. "The bearded fellow dressed in black."

"Not the relevant question," I replied.

"What do you have to say for yourself, Norris?" Holmes asked. "What are you doing here?"

"I want to go with you," the lad proclaimed.

I set my bag down next to Holmes's. "We're going to Liverpool," I said resolutely, assuming he could not possibly be prepared for such an undertaking.

But the young man fooled me. He responded with a broad grin. At the same time, he held up his right hand. Between his thumb and forefinger, he grasped a train ticket for Lime Street Liverpool. "You see, Mr. Holmes," young Norris boasted, "I went to the same wicket you had and asked to buy the same ticket the man in the deerstalker hat had bought."

Very resourceful, I found myself thinking.

"What do you say?" Norris asked Holmes. "I deserve the chance. After all, it was my drawing that got this investigation going in the first place."

"Your mother—" I began.

"I've already sent her a telegram. She's used to me being on my own."

Holmes and I looked at each other in silence. The journey was not without its dangers, but the shrieking whistle from the express required an immediate decision. Holmes shrugged agreement, and we both picked up our Gladstones.

The youthful Norris bounded ahead. "Hurry up!" he shouted over his shoulder, "Or we'll miss our train."

Q

The three of us had a compartment to ourselves. As soon as the train began to roll, Holmes sat back, and though he stared out the window, I recognised the routine. I knew him to be contemplating the logistics of our investigation. Young Frank Norris, on the other hand, sat opposite us, presumably looking at me to initiate conversation. I suspect it required but a few quiet minutes for him to recognise that I had no experience whatsoever in speaking to lads of seventeen.

Once it became apparent that neither Holmes nor I was wont to socialise, Norris produced a book from his haversack. It had a dark-green cover and in gilt-letters displayed the familiar title, *Ivanhoe*.

Something to talk about, I thought with relief. "Excellent novel," I volunteered. "Scott's one of my favourites."

"Mine too. But, you know, Doctor Watson," Norris smiled a bit ruefully, "as much as I love Sir Walter Scott"—he held up the book—"he got the armour very wrong. He was a hundred years off in describing the designs. Why, it would be like putting Richelieu in a top hat and frock coat."

I recalled the intricate drawings of armour in Norris's' sketchpad. "I didn't know that," I said blankly.

With a shrug, Norris began reading. Some ten minutes later, however, he replaced the book and did some more rummaging inside the haversack. On this occasion, he produced a pencil. But rather than the sketchpad I expected to see, he extracted a smaller, leather-bound notebook. I watched him write "Euston Station" at the top of a page and then the date and our time of departure. He added Holmes's name, mine, and his own.

"Not drawing then?" I asked.

Norris smiled. "As an aspiring writer yourself, Doctor, I'm sure you know that you never can tell when you might want a record of what you've been doing. I keep a journal."

"I recall that your mother told us you were interested in writing."

"Yes," the young man said with a wistful smile, "but to be honest, I don't write as much as I draw. From time to time, I add to the historical adventures I began a while ago for my brother Charles. He's got a lot of toy soldiers—thousands of them, or so it seems—and I make up stories about them. Now that Lester is gone and there are just the two of us, I guess I'll have to write some more and send them to him."

"Most considerate," I said.

"To tell you the truth," chuckled Norris, "my stories give me a reason to draw. First, I write; then I create the illustrations. But don't get me wrong. I love doing the pictures. Right now, I think I'm a better artist than a writer."

As luck would have it, the Scottish Highlander still rested in my coat pocket, and I gently withdrew it, leaned forward, and placed it upright on the seat cushion next to Norris. Though the figure wobbled a bit with the motion of the train, it remained standing. "Draw *him*," I suggested.

Norris proceeded to size up the Highlander and minutes later, on a fresh page in his notebook, began to sketch the Scottish soldier. As if drawing allowed him to speak more freely, it was then that he told me about his mother's career on the stage. A quarter of an hour later, he showed me his rendering of my Highland miniature. Like his earlier drawing of the murder scene, he produced a very accurate portrait indeed.

Flashing past our carriage window, the small houses of north London and later the flat, green pastures of farmland provided Norris additional subjects to draw. He worked silently now, and Holmes continued to stare pensively out the window. With no one to speak to, it did not take long for the rhythmic swaying and repetitive clattering of the railway to produce its somnolent effects, and soon enough I was asleep.

In retrospect, I suppose my disturbing dreams were not surprising. Visions of coal pits floated through my anxious brain, their portals opening and closing like giant jaws—some, terrifyingly, lined with fanglike teeth. It was as if I could hear them gnashing when I woke with a start, only to discover that the train was rattling through the station at Stafford. I woke up again as we rolled through Crewe, but managed to doze off once more. When I awoke a third time, I found myself enshrouded in darkness. I could see nothing.

"Where are we?" I asked in confusion.

"In the last tunnel before Lime Street," said Holmes.

I had slept so long that I did not realise we had already traversed most of the narrow corridor of rails that runs beneath the arches, plunges through an assortment of tunnels, and debouches into the Lime

Street Station. Not long thereafter, we rolled to a halt, and the three of us—Gladstones and haversack in hand—disembarked. Minutes later we were walking between the pair of granite columns that marked the exit to the outside world.

On the other side of Lime Street loomed our destination for the night, the imposing five-storey North and Western Hotel, its rounded archway, red-brick façade, and slate roof reminding one of a massive French château. We crossed the road and took young Norris for a meal of fish-and-chips in the hotel's restaurant. Afterwards, I managed to fob the young man off as my son and had him bunk in my room. He slept on the sofa and I on the bed.

The next morning Holmes, Norris, and I passed once more between the station's two columns—"the candlesticks" a clerk in the hotel called them—purchased our tickets, and located the platform for the Wigan branch line. A small locomotive was set to pull a single carriage, and a few minutes after we secured our seats, the train lurched forward, a shrill whistle announcing our departure for the town of Wigan and the expansive South Lancashire coalfields that surround it.

Chapter Ten

The Collieries

... I began to see that a fellow can't live *for* himself any more
than he can live *by* himself. He's got to think of others. If
he's got brains, he's got to think for the poor ducks that
haven't 'em, and not give 'em a boot in the backsides
because they happen to be stupid. . . .

Frank Norris
The Octopus:
A Story of California

*T*he train ride from Liverpool, which lies
some seventeen miles southwest of Wigan, took half
an hour. I expected an ever-bleaker landscape, but
much of the area adjacent to the rails contains a rich
variety of industries, their tall, brick chimneys
marring the blue sky with thick clouds of black
smoke. Among them are foundries, blast furnaces,
rolling mills, chemical plants, and wagon works—
businesses eager to establish themselves where coal
is so readily available.

The coalfields also dictate the network of
railway tracks. The country requires fuel—hence,
the rails providing access throughout the land. The
swing bridges we rattled across served as reminders
that waterways like the nearby River Douglas and the

Sankey Canal serve much the same function in distributing the coal, but on a significantly lesser scale since the coming of the railway.

We arrived mid-morning at Wigan's North Union Station. A cool breeze blew through the abbreviated, peak-roofed platform. Disembarking in so confined a space for so necessary a railway, one need not be a captain of industry to recognise the shortcomings of the station. Why, the single tracks on either side of the building could not possibly meet the demands of all the smoke-belching factories nearby. A plaque announcing that the station had been built almost fifty years before underscored its limitations.

Small though it may have been, North Union Station was not without its surprises. For at the end of the platform, observing us from beneath his black bowler, hands deep in the pockets of his long tan coat, stood the pale-faced Tobias Gregson.

"Inspector," Holmes addressed the policeman who was approaching us. "What are you doing here?"

"I'm waiting for Lestrade to arrive." Gregson seemed genuinely pleased to see familiar faces and eagerly shook hands with Holmes and me. To the young man standing behind us, however, Gregson paid no attention; to Gregson, Norris might as well have been invisible.

"Lestrade's due later this afternoon," Gregson went on. "When he gets here, we'll be off to the Pemberton Mining Office." He pointed at a nearby road. "It's about a mile from here."

"What's there?" I asked.

"I gave descriptions of O'Connor and Worthy to the station master," Gregson said, "and he immediately recognised them. He told me they came in separately some two hours apart. The first one, the one man with a thick moustache, had been carrying a heavy sack."

"O'Connor," I said.

Gregson nodded. "He asked for the nearest mining office, and the station master directed him to Pemberton's up the road."

"Pemberton doesn't figure into this case," Holmes said.

"Agreed," nodded Gregson. "But when Lestrade arrives, we'll go see what we can learn inside the Pemberton office."

"What about the second man?" Holmes wanted to know. "Inspector Worthy, one assumes."

"Correct. He arrived two hours later demanding to know where the first fellow had gone. The station master pointed him in the direction of Pemberton's as well."

Gregson's report accounted for the two men we were tracking, but not for what had summoned the police to Wigan. "What brought you here?" I asked him. "Did you find Worthy's notes when you searched his rooms?"

"No. Nothing there. But with Nigel missing, the Yard issued a look-out for him. Many of our lads know Inspector Worthy personally. A man of his height—well over six feet—is difficult to miss, and so identification was not a problem. In fact, it was a constable on duty at Euston who saw him purchase a ticket.

"The Commissioner cautioned us at the Yard that Worthy is armed and possibly dangerous, so our men were told not to confront him on their own. That's why I'm waiting for Lestrade. In any case, once Nigel had left the ticket window, the constable asked the agent for the destination of the previous traveller. Wigan was the answer, and I was assigned the task of bringing Nigel in."

I felt Norris poke me in the back to be certain I had not missed Gregson's confirmation of the lad's report.

"And Lestrade?" asked Holmes.

"I left word at the Yard that I was following Worthy here. Lestrade and I shared the opinion that if Nigel was in Wigan, one could reasonably assume that O'Connor, the man Nigel was chasing, would be here as well."

"Our thought exactly," said Holmes, "though how Worthy himself knew to come to Wigan remains a mystery."

"Perhaps he simply followed the dentist," I suggested.

"Perhaps," said Holmes though his furrowed brow indicated he did not believe that to be the case.

"Now, gentlemen," said Gregson, "it's my turn to ask you the same question you asked me. How did *you* know to come to Wigan?"

Holmes turned and, urging our young companion forward, introduced him to the Inspector.

"Norris, is it then?" Gregson greeted the lad as if seeing him for the first time. "Inspector Lestrade has spoken of you. Your drawing of the murder scene—quite well done, I'm told."

Norris smiled broadly, apparently never tiring from receiving compliments.

"And yet, Mr. Holmes, you haven't answered my question. What brought you to these coalfields?"

Sherlock Holmes nodded his head at Norris. "Like your constable, this young man was also at Euston when Worthy purchased his ticket. The lad recognised him as the detective at the museum and overheard the clerk tell your constable that Wigan was Worthy's destination. It would appear that we're all in the hunt together."

"But you got here before we did," I said to Gregson, "and we took the express."

"No mystery, there, Doctor. I came on the slow train. Had to change trains in Crewe, but still arrived in Liverpool before the express. Spent the

129

night in a small hotel. The local constabulary brought me here early this morning—police business and all that, don't you know?"

Holmes rubbed his hands together impatiently. "I can understand that *you* have to wait for your colleague, Gregson," he said, "but we have no such responsibility. Watson and I are going after Worthy—and O'Connor too if, as the station master reported, he's here as well."

Gregson was about to say something. I imagine he was going to warn us against getting involved in a police pursuit, but Holmes spoke first. "I do have a favour to ask of you, however," he said. Once again, he turned to our young companion. "I'd like you to look after Mr. Norris."

I was happy to hear Holmes make the request.

"We are about to face danger," Holmes said. "Firearms might be involved, and Watson and I want to keep the boy safe."

Holmes placed a hand on Norris's shoulder, but the lad squirmed out from under it.

"I want to go with you, Mr. Holmes," he said.

"No," Holmes replied firmly, "you're to stay here."

Bolstering Holmes's position, I shook my head at Norris. "Your mother would never forgive us if something happened to you. She's already warned us about keeping you out of trouble. We'll supply you with a full report when we come back."

Now it was Gregson's turn to place his palm on young Norris's shoulder. Though the lad was obviously not under arrest, he still seemed to sense the fabled "heavy hand of the law." With a frown, the young man folded his arms in front of his chest.

At the same time, rumbling by the railway platform was a long, open wagon pulled by two stout, black horses. Its bed was framed with wooden slats, which functioned as seats and—at least, for the moment—happened to be empty.

Holmes hailed the driver, an older fellow with tinted glasses and grey side-whiskers, and asked if he could transport us to the Pemberton Company's office. The driver motioned that we climb aboard, and the two of us hurried from the platform along the cobblestones to where the wagon was standing. The horses snorted impatiently as we hoisted ourselves onto the rudimentary seats. No sooner were we settled than the wagon jerked forward.

Young Frank Norris, arms still folded, watched us trundle off in the direction of the mines.

We entered a wasteland. I know little about the negative glass plates utilised in cameras, except to say that they reverse the gradations of the light and dark colourings of the original image. In short, what

131

is black appears white, and what is white appears black.

The topography around us suggested such a reversal. If one could somehow imagine depicted in shades of inky darkness the light-coloured landscapes we associate with the desolate and cratered moon, one might reasonably elicit the soulless image of the vast Lancashire coalfield lying before us with its man-made wounds and scars.

Not that the blackened terrain was flat. On the contrary, pockmarked as it was by small pools of murky water, the prospect, replete with rotted tree-stumps and leafless snags, was more dramatically interrupted by a random assortment of wood and metal structures that towered above the open pits—"headframes" our driver called them—employed to accommodate pulleys and windlasses.

Nor was it quiet. All manner of machinery contributed to a cacophony of metallic dissonance: the grinding of powerful drills, the roar of hydraulic monitors, the pounding of stamp-mills and crushers—all punctuated by intermittent explosions of dynamite.

Our driver pointed out the pit-banks where coal was sorted, the excavations where slag heaps were formed, and the piles of gravel where railway ballast was produced. With the sweep of his hand, he indicated the small-gauge rails linking various pits and the planked footpaths— "boardwalks," the

Americans call them—connecting a string of simple wooden buildings.

It was a foreign world through which we travelled, and we felt much relieved when deposited in front of a conventional-looking outhouse, a small, low structure that served as an office. The wood sign above the door read: *Pemberton Colliery Co.*

Thanks to a pot-bellied stove at the back of the room, a welcome rush of warm air enveloped us as soon as we entered. A balding clerk in shirtsleeves was marking in some sort of account book at a table that faced the door. Upon hearing us walk in, he looked up with a scowl, his round, wire-rimmed glasses reflecting the sunlight pouring through the small windows on either side of the door.

The room itself contained three major pieces of furniture: an open, cherrywood roll-top desk to our right, the pine table directly in front of us at which the clerk was sitting, and behind the table a solid-looking bookshelf jammed with mining paraphernalia—helmets, lanterns and such.

Unfurled across the desktop and marked in blue ink lay a large, rectangular map. Prevented from curling by an additional pair of rolled maps placed upon its edges, the open map appeared to depict the adjacent coalfields.

Nor was the clerk alone. At the ceiling in the corner of the room nearest the desk, there depended from a metal hook and slender chain a tall, gilt birdcage occupied by a chittering yellow canary. When the bird fluttered about, the cage swung ever-so-slightly back and forth like a slow-moving pendulum. In addition, on the floor near the stove lay a large grey puppy, possibly a Great Dane.

The clerk coughed as we approached, and the puppy raised its large head. "Yes?" the fellow asked sharply, obviously annoyed at being disturbed. "What do you want?" He cleared his throat whilst carefully looking us over. If he had reached some sort of judgment, it did not feel positive.

"We're searching for two men who came in here a few hours ago," Holmes answered. "They weren't together, but we need to know if you saw them."

The clerk shut the account book and, rubbing his right palm over his shiny head, exhaled loudly. "The penalty for working in the office closest to the station," he sighed. "People come in with all sorts of questions." He coughed again, then announced abruptly, "Yes, I saw them, the both of them—two tall men."

"Those are the ones," I said.

"I remember the first one in particular—thick yellow moustache; curly blond hair. Black stocking cap. He was breathing heavily—probably from the weight of the bag he was carrying. Hard to believe, but when he set it down, it sounded like it was full of coins."

"What did they want?" Holmes asked.

In spite of his irritability, the fellow seemed more than eager to furnish information—a way of being done with us, I reckoned.

"They wanted to know the name of a pit that's shut down. No, wait. That's not quite right. The first bloke, he knew the name: Goshawk No. 1. He just wanted to be sent in the right direction. There's lots of deserted pits, you know. Goshawk's not one of ours, but when you're here long enough, you learn the history."

"Did he say why he was looking for that particular mine?" Holmes asked.

Coughing again, the clerk could only nod in confirmation. After a few more hacks, he said, "He told me his father worked that mine when this fellow was a lad. Said he himself was a car-boy in it, but hadn't been back in over twenty years. 'Things are laid out different,' he said, 'new buildings and the like.'" There followed a wet, ropy cough. Longer than the previous two, it overpowered the canary's song. As it went on, the grey puppy rose and sidled over to the desk, and the clerk obligingly rubbed its ears.

Holmes leaned towards him. "And the second fellow?"

The clerk looked up from the dog. "The one in the long coat and bowler," he said, peering at us over the narrow rim of his glasses. "He didn't know the name of the pit, but then he wasn't looking for it. He said he was looking for the first fellow, so I sent him over to Goshawk No. 1 as well."

"Where is this Goshawk No. 1?" I asked.

"Out the door and turn right," the clerk said, his hands pointing the direction. "Then go about a mile along the wooden footpath. When you get to the rusted remains of a headframe, turn left, and you'll see the entrance. It's boarded up now, but I shouldn't imagine that will keep you out. Be warned though. Have care when you get inside. There are cracks and holes and falling rocks. It's not safe to be wandering about in there."

We prepared to leave, but unlike the only other man we encountered in our investigations who owned yellow birds—the villain called Wilson whom I would dub "the notorious canary trainer"*— the clerk exhibited a degree of sympathy. "Wait," he added and turning round, proceeded to reach among the lanterns on the shelf behind him. "Take a couple of these," he said and gave a lantern to each of us.

The lanterns were unusual. Each had a familiar, large-ringed handle at its top, but their open wicks were surrounded by wire mesh.

---

* Watson mentions this case in the adventure he titled "Black Peter." Adrian Conan Doyle, Sir Arthur's son, published a version of Wilson's villainy in a sketch titled "The Adventure of the Deptford Horror."

"They're Davy lamps," the clerk explained. "You'll need them in the mine. I gave a couple to those other fellows as well. The lamps won't light up much, but they'll help you get about. The mesh prevents the flame from escaping and igniting any gases in the air. Need matches?"

"No," Holmes said, patting his waistcoat pocket. "I've got my own."

"Light them before you go in. That mine may be closed down, but we still don't want any explosions. It happened once; it can happen again. That's the thing about a pit—working or shut down. You never know. . . ."

On that ominous note, Holmes and I took our leave. Following the clerk's instructions, we headed off into the cool air and turned right. We closed the door behind us as we left, and whilst we could no longer hear the chirping of the canary, we could still make out the coughs. Moments later, however, our footfalls on the wooden footpath drowned out the last of the sounds from the office.

Colliers scuttled into and out of the dark pit-entrances like worker-ants negotiating their nests. Some guided the mules that hauled the coal bins to waiting wagons; others carried the heavy sacks themselves, bent low as they trudged along. Yet all bore stoic—dare I say, "heroic"?—faces smeared with the blackened grit of coal dust, testimony to the exhausting labour so necessary for heating all the homes of England.

Our observations were not merely sympathetic, however. On the trail of a killer, we had to assume that the rogue could secretly be marking our own advancement just as we sought his. Behind any shed or outhouse might be lurking the miscreant who would go to the greatest of extremes to keep us, as well as the police, from apprehending him. And so we proceeded cautiously upon the planks.

To our great relief, we reached the skeletal remains of the headframe by the side of the boardwalk without incident. As the clerk had told us, in the ground some twenty paces to our left appeared the large, partially boarded entrance to the mine shaft. Beside the opening stood a warped wood sign whose faded letters were barely visible. *Goshawk No. 1*, it read.

Splintered wood-struts framed the entrance, and there still remained a number of horizontal planks that at one time had sealed off the excavation. No doubt the planks were installed after the mine had become unusable—probably, to judge from the ancient rubble near the entrance, ever since the cave-in that had killed O'Connor's father years before. None the less, enough of the boards were missing or pushed aside to allow entrance though a veil of darkness concealed whatever mysteries lay below.

Behind the *Goshawk* sign sat a rusted cage, a useless appendage of the dilapidated headframe. The cage appeared to be part of a small lift, which had been raised and lowered by means of a pulley and winch, their rusted remains lying a few yards from the pit.

"Note the rope," Holmes said, pointing to a cable tied to the base of the winch. The other end dangled down into the darkness of the mine's entrance. He picked up a stone and leaning over the opening, dropped it into the pit. A moment later, the stone hit the bottom, and Holmes said, "About thirty feet down, I should judge," He pulled up the rope to examine its length. "This should be satisfactory. What's more, whoever last used it must still be down there, or else one assumes it would have been pulled up."

To free his left hand for the descent, Holmes slipped his left forearm through the large ring at the top of his lantern, picked up the rope with his right, and throwing the line over his shoulder, shuffled backwards towards the opening. He gave the rope a few strong tugs to assure himself it would hold, and then, with the lantern on his arm and his feet braced against the dirt wall, he proceeded to lower himself hand-below-hand into the darkness like an experienced alpinist. A minute or so later I heard his muffled voice shouting up from below: "Your turn, Watson."

Not that I looked forward to the descent, but I followed Holmes's actions and with some effort managed to brace my legs against the top of the mineshaft wall and in as close an imitation of Holmes as I could muster, lower myself into the void.

The drop was considerable—though lesser, I have since been told, than in most other pits. Still, due to the twofold pressure—on my shoulder and my legs—the exertion caused me great discomfort as it resurrected the forgotten pains of my old war wound. The fear of falling helped concentrate my efforts, however, and with the greatest of caution, I successfully negotiated my descent to the floor of the mine.

Once safely down, I could see that the area was not totally dark. Sunlight shone through the opening above, and additional slivers of light streaked the walls where splits and spaces between the remaining planks above us allowed the beams to penetrate. But thanks to the massive earthen walls, not the noise. For the moment, at least, stillness reigned—though soured by the dank odours of methane, moist earth, and ancient mule droppings that filled the close and heavy air.

Fortunately, there was sufficient light to reveal at our feet the remnants of the rails for the old coal bins pulled by mules—rusted, small-gauge tracks that led from where we were standing into an uninviting corridor of blackness. As we peered ahead, Holmes withdrew the match box from his waistcoat.

"The clerk said to light the lamps before we went in," I reminded my friend.

"Too late now, I'm afraid," Holmes shrugged and, nodding his head to reassure me all would be well, struck a Vesta.

I swallowed hard, but nothing exploded, and Holmes went on to light both lamps. However feeble the illumination, we could see where the rails were leading and as a consequence dared to take a few halting steps forward.

As we progressed, the lanterns helped us discern our surroundings. Set every few feet in the earthen walls, vertical posts and cross-beams valiantly held up what was left of a ridged metal ceiling—though, in truth, many of the metal sheets lay on the blackened floor about us. Here and there a discarded coat or shirt or the odd boot rested haphazardly against the base of a sidewall. Gingerly, we stepped over the remains of any such debris, and only at the slowest pace did we wend our way forward along the rails, feeling more than seeing that the sinuous path was descending in a kind of natural staircase.

We passed a shaft for ventilation though the farther we walked, the more we encountered newer smells of spent dynamite and burnt rubber. We had little sense of where we were going or even if the people we were seeking were actually inside—until quite literally, we stumbled over a clue.

I kicked away a bowler that had been lying on the path. Holmes pointed to the hat as it rolled atop a discarded shirt at the base of the wall next to us. Holding my lamp above the debris, I also saw a torn coat and a ragged pair of dungarees.

"What do you make of it?" Holmes asked.

I thought for a moment. We had seen discarded clothing before. Most of the articles looked as if they belonged to the miners, but a bowler seemed out of place in a coal pit. Then again, various mining agents might come down to check on conditions.

"Well?" said Holmes.

"It probably belonged to some sort of supervisor," I offered, "maybe a union boss."

"To a great mind," Holmes replied, "nothing is little."

Some other individual might have felt complimented by those words. I, on the other hand, recognised their provenance. Holmes had uttered them sententiously the first time I heard them, and he spoke them sententiously now. They were the same words he had directed at Gregson upon the Inspector's discovery of another hat, that one in the Lauriston Gardens murder case. Gregson had thought it a significant clue, but it turned out to be the proverbial red herring. Holmes's remark had been inflated mockery. It was my turn now to feel the sting.

"Pick up the hat, old fellow," he said, "and tell me what you observe."

Although it was a black bowler like countless others one sees in London every day, I lifted it and, turning the hat upside down, examined the leather band within. Holmes held his lamp close by, so we simultaneously discovered the initials *N.W.* stamped into the leather. Presumably, I was holding the bowler worn by Nigel Worthy.

"But how did you know?" I asked Holmes. "You couldn't see the band."

"Note the fine ridges on the crown, Watson. They're indicative of a rigid network made of cane that protects one's head. Worthy is a prudent fellow. He had his bowler lined like a constable's helmet. His initials merely confirm our suspicions."

I nodded, buoyed by the added incentive of knowing we were in the right place.

Holmes and I pushed on.

Some ten feet later, the rails ended, and the dark, narrow tunnel fanned out into a spacious, cavelike structure whose farther end was lost somewhere in the shadows. By then, I reckoned we had penetrated a half-mile into the mine.

"This must be where the wall and ceiling gave way," Holmes observed. "Hence, the cavern—however far it extends."

In the larger area, the air felt lighter, and the Davy lamps illuminated enough to reveal that we no longer stood inside a confining tunnel, but on a narrow ledge, all that remained after the cave-in of the walls. In fact, Holmes and I stood dangerously close to a precipice whose drop-off I had no desire to sample.

Once more Holmes dropped a stone and listened for the impact. Moments passed, and he said, "Well over fifty feet I should judge."

"Small wonder the work ended," I said. "This place became a death-trap."

The two of us stood silently staring at the precariousness of our position.

Suddenly, the quiet was interrupted.

"Far enough!" a hollow voice commanded. "I have a gun," the final word resounding over and over again from somewhere off in the darkness.

Holmes and I raised our lanterns in the futile hope of extending our vision. Some thirty feet in front of us on the narrow ledge, we could barely make out the figure of what appeared to be a very large man. Whoever he was, his arm was pointing in our direction, and in his hand was a pistol. It was aimed directly at Holmes and me.

Chapter Eleven

On the Edge

You can fancy [a gun's] birth
in the forge in the midst of fire and molten ore;
then its first shot and the certain grim quiver of joy
running through its brazen loins with the recoil,
when the savage, huge life is unleashed
in a roar and a red flame.
--Frank Norris
"With the Peacemakers"

Worthy or O'Connor? In the surrounding darkness, I could not be certain. The hulking form could belong to either man. The voice sounded muffled, and I slipped my hand in my pocket to feel the comfort of my Webley. It was dark enough, I thought, to withdraw the pistol without being seen.

"I'm trapped here," the disembodied voice shouted. "I can't get out." Enriched by the slowly diminishing echo, the cry sounded all the more plaintive.

As I pondered the cause of his lament, the speaker struck a match, and I removed my hand from the Webley so as not to provoke him. The light was minimal, but it was sufficient to illuminate our antagonist. Though he appeared slighter than I

147

remembered, I recognised beneath the black knitted cap the square jaw and thick moustache of Liam O'Connor, the dentist, who was now barring our way. On the ground behind him lay the canvas sack. It looked quite full.

In the flare of the match, however, there was more to see. Next to O'Connor on the narrow ground above the precipice, the flickering light revealed the cause of his entrapment. Beside a pair of extinguished Davy lamps lay the inert form of Inspector Nigel Worthy. He appeared to be unconscious, if not already dead. And yet one could not fail to note that as O'Connor moved his right arm, so also moved the left arm of the man lying beside him. The clink of a metal chain accompanied the movement.

"They're handcuffed together," Holmes whispered.

I could now see for myself that attached at their wrists as the two figures were, the weight of Worthy's body prevented O'Connor from moving in either direction along the narrow path. As the dentist had rightly said, he was indeed trapped.

"Enough sympathy for the devil," I said to myself and focused my concern on the unfortunate Worthy. How well he wore that name! One could scarcely imagine the policeman's heroism—to have the courage not only to follow O'Connor down into the pit but then to go after him into the darkness, handcuff the man, and attempt to bring him in. Such resolve required a tenacity and nerve not generally seen in most people, not even in policemen. A wave of remorse rushed over me as I realised how we had doubted him. And now we did not know whether he was alive or dead.

"Where's the key, man?" Holmes demanded of the dentist, the echo highlighting the question.

"You think I haven't thought of that?" O'Connor said. "It's down below somewhere— wherever the copper threw it. He claimed I murdered Katherine. I thought he was my friend, but he drew his gun and tried to arrest me right here.

"Well, I'd have none of it, and I leapt at him and grabbed his gun. We struggled and the thing— this one—" he held up the pistol, "it went off. The fool was struck by his own bullet. As he fell, I grabbed the gun, but somehow he managed to cuff the both of us and toss the key over the edge. And then he died."

"Are you certain he's dead?" I asked.

"I know when someone's dead," O'Connor proclaimed. "I'm a dentist." Then, his tone laced with sarcasm, he sputtered, "or used to be. I guess we're both done for now."

The echo trailed off, and silence marked the finality of it all, a silence intensified by the dead world surrounding us.

Holmes interrupted the stillness. "And did you?" he asked.

"Did I what?"

"Murder your wife?"

O'Connor paused a moment, then said, "I suppose I did. It doesn't matter now."

We could barely see him, but I imagined his face appearing lined and gaunt. The dentist pointed to the canvas bag by his side. "She wouldn't hand it over, so I took it. It's all I really wanted. If she'd only given it to me, everything would be different."

"What did you do?" Holmes asked.

"I found her in the museum. It was after hours, and I pounded on the door. She opened it a crack to see who was there, and I pushed my way in and demanded the money. She said she wouldn't give it to me. She said it was all hers. I told her, 'You can't make small of me,' and I punched her in the face. She didn't go down, so I hit her again in the side of her head and left her on the floor.

"I figured I'd done her then, but I didn't care. Many was the time I said I'd make her dance. I went back to her room and searched the place without her bloody nagging. This time I found the loose floorboard under the bed where she kept the gold, and I took it all. Put it in that bag."

To point at the sack, he raised his wrist, the one linked to Worthy's, and the dead policeman's arm rose as well. The dentist uttered a stifled laugh. "I guess it won't help me now."

"Why did you come *here*?" Holmes asked.

"I grew up in this pit," said the dentist. "I know the mine. Used to come in with my dad. I was a car-boy back then. I figured the old Goshawk was as safe a place to hide as anywhere else. Except that I forgot I'd told Nigel about it."

That's how Worthy knew to come to Wigan, I realised.

Just then, footsteps and familiar voices sounded behind us. Gregson and Lestrade had obviously talked to the clerk in the colliery office and learned where we had gone and figured how to make the descent into the mine. Emerging flickers of light told us that they too had been given Davy lamps.

"The police have arrived," Holmes told O'Connor. "You can let them unlock the manacles and take you in or stay here forever chained to a dead man."

As Gregson and Lestrade were joining us on the narrow path, O'Connor was hanging his head. "Get me out of here," was all he said.

"First, Worthy's gun," Holmes demanded. "Place it on the ground and use your foot to slide it in our direction."

Gregson was about to speak, but Holmes raised his hand for silence.

Meanwhile, O'Connor did as instructed, gently kicking the gun towards us with his huge right boot.

The pistol appeared to be an Adams or an Enfield. In the darkness I could not tell for certain.

"Don't move!" Holmes said. "Help is coming." He then turned to the two policemen and quickly informed them of the situation.

It was Gregson who stepped up—like Worthy, a man of courage. Placing his lantern on the ground as well as his bowler, he moved forward on the narrow ledge and, stooping to pick up the gun, placed it in the pocket of his tan coat. Then he drew a key from his waistcoat and inched forward until he reached the dentist. He stooped again and removed the cuff from the dead Inspector's wrist. I assumed it was his intention to manacle both of O'Connor's wrists together, but Gregson never got the chance.

Once free from Worthy, the dentist used his powerful car-boy's hands to push Gregson backward against the earthen wall. With the chain still dangling from his right wrist, O'Connor picked up the canvas bag, turned round to face the abyss, and then, without another word, leapt into the darkness, hugging the sack as he fell. There was no scream or shout, just the sickening thud of his body—along with the cascading ring of a shower of sovereigns—all hitting the rocky floor of the coal pit at the same time.

"O'Connor?" Holmes shouted.

No answer but the echo.

"O'Connor?" he shouted once more.

Again, the echo—and then only silence.

Gregson scrambled to his feet and recovered his lantern. Then, along with Lestrade, Holmes, and me, he raised his Davy lamp high over the edge of the precipice. But O'Connor had fallen so far that not even the four lamps held together could generate enough light to illuminate the scene.

Moments later, the crunch of new footfalls announced more company, and young Norris came towards us on the ledge. Somewhere he had found an actual torch, which was now alight and better—if not more dangerously—illuminating the area. Observing us holding our lanterns over the side of the footpath, he brandished his flame there as well.

In the glow of the dancing fire, we could now distinguish the remains of Liam O'Connor. Atop a pile of black rocks far below, his broken body lay twisted in the centre of a pool of golden coins, each one flickering and winking as it caught the light from Norris's torch.

"You there," exclaimed Gregson to young Norris, "what are you doing here? We told you not to follow us." Clearly, Gregson was not used to being disobeyed.

"We left him in the mining office," Lestrade explained, "with the clerk and the dog."

"And the canary," Norris was quick to add.

Gregson glared at the lad, but Sherlock Holmes placed a calming hand on the Inspector's arm.

"Right then," said Lestrade, attempting to return to business. "We'll need to get the locals to take these bodies out and collect the money." Perhaps, in appreciation of Gregson's brave interaction with O'Connor, he added, "I'll arrange it."

An appeased Gregson brushed some coal dust off his tan coat and replaced his bowler. "An ugly business," he said, shaking his head. He then joined Lestrade, and the two of them, continuing to hold their lamps aloft, strode off together in the same direction from where we had all entered the pit.

"The man down there was a dentist," Norris said when the three of us were alone. "Isn't that right?"

"Indeed," Holmes replied.

"One who had no licence and lost his way," I added.

"But a murderer just the same," the lad said, shaking his head. "It is astounding, is it not? A man with a reputation, with an income, with a wife . . . and that"—he held the torch over the spot where O'Connor's body now lay—"is what he turned into."

"Or already was from the start," I suggested.

Young Norris stared down into the chasm. "Please, give me a moment," he said. As he spoke,

154

he withdrew from his jacket the small black notebook and pencil. Then, without asking, he proceeded to toss the torch down into the pit where it landed not far from the dentist. One could hear the jingle of coins as the torch struck the earth. Continuing to burn, it illuminated the scene brightly enough for Norris to draw.

Holding our lanterns high in a meagre attempt to help the lad see his work, Holmes and I watched silently as he began to sketch. Granted the time was hurried, but in the dim light of our Davy lamps we could see taking shape the blackened rocks, the flaming torch, the shining gold sovereigns, and the twisted body at the centre. In what literary critics like to call "full circle," its composition—a corpse (though minus the two policemen)—very much recalled the drawing with which this investigation had commenced.

Propping our legs against the wall of the pit and pulling the rope taut, the three of us in turn managed to hoist ourselves up and out of the mine. We hailed a wagon, which transported us back to the Wigan train station. On the road, we passed Lestrade and a team of constables heading in the other direction. They were going to Goshawk No. 1 to collect the two bodies and gather the coins.

The night train from Liverpool returned Holmes, Norris and me to Euston Station. During the journey I detailed for young Frank the events that had led to the tragedy he had depicted in his drawing— O'Connor's lust, Katherine's greed, and Worthy's heroism.

As I spoke, Norris wrote in his notebook, "Ideas for a possible story." He added his name a few inches below.

"An excellent plan," the writer within me responded. Here was an opportunity to encourage the writer inside of him. "You've already criticised Sir Walter Scott," I said. "Perhaps you're ready to try your own hand at constructing a novel."

Norris chewed on the end of his pencil. "You never know," he said. "If it's no good, I can give it to my brother Charles. I don't expect him to complain. He's a willing audience."

"I have faith in you," I told him. "Any help I might have to offer, don't hesitate to ask."

The boy busied himself writing for much of the rest of our journey. Though I could not read his neat but tiny script, I did notice the large, block letters that headed his first blank page: "The Dentist." To me, it seemed he had already settled on the title for his novel.

Upon arriving in London, we secured a cab to return Norris to the Morley and ourselves to Baker Street. Suffice it to say that we arrived back at our digs in time for a late breakfast of eggs and bacon served by Billy under orders from Mrs. Hudson. But it was our landlady herself who delivered the coffee.

Though I need not report on the poor souls we observed sleeping on benches or roaming the streets that early morning, I do confess to sympathizing with them more than I ever had before.

Chapter Twelve

Dénouement

"Murder and sudden death," say you?
Yes, but it's the life that lives;
it's reality, it's the thing that counts.
--Frank Norris
"An Opening for Novelists"

"*M*rs. Norris and son to see you both," announced Billy at the end of the week. It was late in the morning, and Holmes and I had no expectation of entertaining visitors.

"Show them in," Holmes said as the two of us shrugged into our jackets.

Yet again, Gertrude Norris, still in black, swept into our sitting room, young Frank trailing in her wake. To my astonishment—and much to Holmes's amusement—upon his head Norris sported a deer-stalker.* Draped over his shoulders was a long tweed coat. *The son of an actress*, I mused.

---

* To those who might suspect Watson of romanticizing Norris's appearance, Franklin Walker assures us on page 49 of *Frank Norris: A Biography*, that "occasionally [Norris] even wore a 'Sherlock Holmes' cap."

"Gentlemen, gentlemen," she said, her arms outstretched as if ready to embrace the world. "We wanted to offer our thanks to you for helping Frankie take his mind off the loss of his dearly departed brother." She patted her bosom to emphasise her appreciation. "Tell them, Frankie."

"Yes, thank you," the lad said albeit reluctantly.

"It is we who should be thanking you, Frank," said Holmes. He walked over to his desk and withdrew from it the original drawing the young man had made of the dead woman in the museum. "I promised I'd return it," he said. "Much easier this way than trying to locate you in Paris."

"Thank you, Mr. Holmes," the lad said, "but why don't you keep it? I have the one I drew in the coal mine."

"Yes, indeed, Mr. Holmes," said his mother, ever the artistic promoter—or, at least, the enthusiastic promoter of her son. "You could frame the drawing and consider it a Frank Norris original." She peered round the sitting room. "It would go well on that wall next to the picture of the Arab fellow in the fez."

The "Arab fellow" in question was in reality Major-General Charles George Gordon. It was his death at the hands of the Mahdi in Khartoum two years earlier that prompted me to display his portrait.

"You already know," added Mrs. Norris, "that Frank will be attending the *Académie Julian* in Paris. But after that? Well, who can tell where his art may take him? All I'm saying is that you should hang on to that drawing he gave you. It might be extremely valuable one day."

"Quite the artist," I observed, assuming it more than likely that Norris's drawing of a woman's corpse would end up in one of Holmes's commonplace books rather than on our wall.

"Yes, indeed," Mrs. Norris said, "he is quite the artist." She smiled broadly, then added, "but I trust you won't forget his literary skills either. Frankie tells me that you've been encouraging the boy, Doctor—for which I thank you. Though he may be preoccupied with his art right now, never say that a mother doesn't dream of seeing her son's written work appearing in print—not to mention the very name she blessed him with."

"The name *we* blessed him with, you mean," came a deep voice from a figure standing at our doorway.

"B.F." said Mrs. Norris. Turning to us, she explained, "My husband."

A stocky gentleman in a smart, three-piece, navy suit marched into the room. His limp favoured the angry hip to which young Frank had alerted us.

Removing an unlit cigar from his lips, B.F. Norris directed his words to his wife and son. "The

161

clerk at the Morley told me you'd be here," he said. "I came to collect the both of you. Enough of this murder business, Frank. If you want a career as an artist, it's time to get moving. Time to pack and head for the Continent."

No one offered introductions, and the poor young man, his face flushed, said nothing.

"All right then," proclaimed Gertrude Norris, springing to her feet. She took hold of her husband's arm and reached for her son's shoulder before announcing, "We're off."

And then the three of them disappeared into the hallway.

Q

A letter from Paris arrived in late November. Replete with misspellings, missing upper-case letters, and omitted full stops (typical, I would learn later), the letter turned out to be the last communication I would receive from Frank Norris until his query seven years later regarding the murder of the dentist's wife. Though the young man was off studying in Paris, he had somehow secured a copy of the new *Beeton's Christmas Annual,* the one containing my first published Sherlock Holmes adventure, *A Study in Scarlet.*

I read the letter aloud to Holmes, excluding the errors. "Well done, Doctor," Norris had written in praise of my narrative. "I especially like the American connection and the descriptions of Utah. I expect to read many more of your histories featuring Sherlock Holmes. Your exciting account presents quite the competitive challenge. Who knows? Someday I might just try my own hand at dramatizing the adventure we all so recently shared together."

Sherlock Holmes raised his eyebrows. "Just what the world needs," he said, "yet another Boswell to record my cases. It is obvious, old fellow, that you have rivals lurking about."

Norris concluded his letter in that American way of wishing us both a "Merry Christmas" (rather than a "happy" one). He signed his name "the Boy-Zola."

I should have understood the implications of Norris's self-appointed sobriquet even then. I should have recognised in his mildly amusing reference to M. Zola the dark undertone that he planned to employ in fictionalizing the investigation we had just completed. But, alas, I did not.

I believed that the heroism of Inspector Nigel Worthy would be obvious to all. A victim of my own *naïveté,* I could not imagine that one could retell the story even in fiction without creating an *homage* to the man's courage. Instead of worrying, however, I joined Holmes in raising a glass of amontillado to the

auspicious literary future of the young American
then studying art in Paris.

Epilogue

The larger view always
and through all shams, all wickednesses,
discovers the Truth that will, in the end, prevail,
and all things, surely, inevitably, resistlessly
work together for good.
--Frank Norris
The Octopus:
A Story of California

*F*ollowing the resolution of the murder in the South Kensington Museum of Art and the deaths in the coal pits of Wigan, neither Holmes nor I ever saw Frank Norris again. To be sure, we followed his exploits reporting the Boer War in South Africa and the Spanish-American War in Cuba.*

---

* Norris crossed paths with other American war correspondents whom Holmes and Watson would meet in London some years later—in particular, Richard Harding Davis and the late Stephen Crane. Davis, who, like Norris, wrote of the conflict in South Africa, participated in a murder investigation Watson called *The London Particular*. Crane, who, like Norris, reported events of the Spanish-American War, was involved in the case titled *The Baron of Breed Place*. In addition, although he wasn't a war correspondent, Jack London worked in the laundry of the exclusive Belmont Academy where ten years earlier, Frank Norris had attended school. Watson wrote of meeting London in the case Watson titled *The Outrage at the Diogenes Club*.

In spite of the journalistic endeavours that served to put Norris in harm's way, however, most readers appreciate the writer for his works of fiction. In particular, it is his novels that have earned Frank Norris the highest praise.

In fact, one need search no farther than the words of my own literary agent, Sir Arthur Conan Doyle, to discover the most objective assessment of Norris's strength as a novelist. After all, through Conan Doyle's writings—not to mention his success in representing authors like myself—Sir Arthur is firmly ensconced in the British literary scene.

What is more, having read my personal account of the South Kensington murder and its aftermath in Wigan, Conan Doyle fully recognised the instrumental roles Holmes and I played in resolving the case. As a result, Conan Doyle also understood just how much Norris had distorted reality in his fictionalised version of the crimes.

Knowledge of the truth, however, did nothing to restrain Conan Doyle's unbridled endorsement of Norris's literary talent. On the contrary, such knowledge may have actually increased my agent's appreciation of it. Recording events as they actually happen may be of paramount importance to chronologists like myself, but when writing fiction as Conan Doyle so often does, the ability to manipulate the truth matters most.

Whatever the catalyst, Conan Doyle forwarded to me a copy of the enthusiastic letter he had sent to Grant Richards, Norris's British publisher, comments made public in June of 1899 in the San Francisco paper, *The Wave*, concerning the narrative that Norris had originally planned on titling *The Dentist* (as I had anticipated) but eventually decided to call *McTeague*.

It is a letter that stands as the final judgment—at least, in these pages—not only of the novel based on our murder investigation, but also of Frank Norris himself, its creator, whose early death cut short a most promising literary career.

"What I think," Conan Doyle (not yet *Sir* Arthur in '99) wrote to Richards, "is that you have got the great American Novelist and I am not sure that you have not got the great American novel. It is tremendously good—splendid—and if it does not sell at once must have a steady demand. Such a book cannot go under. I would not alter a word."

Three years after reading Conan Doyle's praise of Frank Norris, Holmes and I raised another glass of amontillado in Norris's honour. On this occasion, however, it was not to pay tribute to his literary future, but to honour the memory of a gifted and talented young man.

THE END

Editor's Notes

To appreciate fully the differences between Dr. Watson's presentation of the murderous events and their interpretation by Frank Norris, one must, of course, read Norris's celebrated novel, *McTeague*. Ironically, despite Arthur Conan Doyle's suggestion to British editor Grant Richards not to alter a word of the book, Richards did in fact make changes in Norris's original manuscript before its British publication, omitting what Richards deemed offensive language.

In addition to Norris's novel, interested readers seeking other interpretations of the story are encouraged to watch *Greed*, Erich von Stroheim's silent movie based on Norris's book. Various edited versions of the original nine-hour film are available online, as are excerpts from the American opera *McTeague* composed by William Bolcom, featuring a libretto by Arnold Weinstein and Robert Altman.

For comprehensive biographies of Frank Norris, see *Frank Norris: A Life* by Joseph R. McElrath, Jr., and Jesse S. Crisier and *Frank Norris Revisited* by Joseph R. McElrath, Jr.

Although outdated, Franklin Walker's *Frank Norris: A Biography* contains numerous insightful anecdotes including the already mentioned news that Frank occasionally wore a "Sherlock Holmes" cap. (It should be pointed out, however, that even with the detail about the deerstalker, none of these biographies mentions the time young Frank spent with Holmes and Watson in England.)

Norris's younger brother Charles, a novelist himself, wrote what he termed "an intimate sketch" of Frank titled *Frank Norris, 1870-1902*.

Though unrelated to the South Kensington murder investigation, Norris's biographers offer a number of interesting stories relevant to Norris's experiences at the University of California when early versions of *McTeague* were percolating in his imagination. McElrath and Crisier report that while a member of the Phi Gamma Delta fraternity, Norris was involved in a dinner-prank the night before Thanksgiving, which involved kissing a pig. So popular was the event, including the reading of a comedic poem written in 1900 by Norris titled "An Exile's Toast" and presented with a German accent that the humorous ceremony evolved into an annual affair at "Fiji" houses throughout the country. Following

Norris's death, the dinner became known as "The Norris."

Ironically, though criticized for his notorious anti-Semitic tropes in *McTeague,* (critic Elisa New called Zerkow, the Zahrkoff character, "the most horrifying Jew in American literature"), Norris was almost not accepted into Phi Gamma Delta because of his association with Jews. Norris and two Jewish friends in particular—Myron Wolf and Maurice V. Samuels—were close enough companions to call themselves "The Three Guardsmen" (according to Walker) or "The Three Musketeers" (according to McElrath and Crisier).

In "The Artist in Frank Norris" (*Pacific Monthly,* March 1907), writer Denison Hailey Clift suggests that Norris, like a few modern film directors—Alfred Hitchcock, most famously—was not beyond inserting himself into his own work. In *McTeague,* Clift identifies Norris in the gold-mining office as the "tall, lean young man, with a thick head of hair surprisingly gray [which Holmes and Watson never had the opportunity to see], who was playing with a half-grown Great Dane puppy." Though Clift may not have known about the dog in Wigan, he does maintain that the office is set in Placer County, California, the "very room," according to Clift, in which "the closing chapters of *McTeague* were written." (Charles Norris considered Frank's placement of himself in the novel an example of his brother's "whimsical humor.")

For further insight into the construction of *McTeague*, readers may consult the *McTeague*-related compositions that Frank Norris wrote in his Harvard writing classes. Many are collected in *A Novelist in the Making: A Collection of Student Themes and the Novels* Blix *and* Vandover and the Brute, edited by James D. Hart. Hart also provides an example of what he terms Norris's "youthful playfulness" in reporting that dental appointments in *McTeague* correspond to the same hours that Professor Gates' writing classes met in the fall of 1894 at Harvard.

For readers interested in the railroad systems in the relevant geographical areas appearing in Dr. Watson's account, see *The North West*, Volume 10 of *A Regional History of the Railways of Great Britain; The Wigan Branch Railway* by Dennis Sweeney; and *Crewe to Carlisle* by Brian Reed.